READ ALOUD LIBRARY
This book belongs to:

An Illustrated Treasury of
READ-ALOUD MYTHS AND LEGENDS

An Illustrated Treasury of

READ-ALOUD MYTHS AND LEGENDS

The World's Best-Loved Myths
and Legends for Parent and Child to Share

EDITED BY JOAN C. VERNIERO AND
ROBIN FITZSIMMONS

BLACK DOG
& LEVENTHAL
PUBLISHERS
NEW YORK

Published by
Black Dog & Leventhal Publishers, Inc.
151 West 19th Street
New York, NY 10011

Distributed by
Workman Publishing Company
708 Broadway
New York, NY 10003

Manufactured in Thailand

Cover and interior design by Liz Driesbach

Cover illustration courtesy Mary Evans Picture Library

ISBN: 1-57912-361-9

h g f e d c b a

Library of Congress Cataloging-in-Publication Data available on file.

Contents

GREEK MYTHS

ROMAN MYTHS

CELTIC MYTHS

SCANDINAVIAN MYTHS

OTHER MYTHS

READ-ALOUD MYTHS AND LEGENDS
Greek Myths

The Adventures of Odysseus

The Greek hero Odysseus was famous for his great skills as a fighter during the Trojan War. It was Odysseus who built the Trojan Horse, a hollow wooden replica of a soldier's steed, in which members of the Greek army hid and surprised the Trojans. He is also well-known for his many adventures during his journey home to the island of Ithaca. In Roman literature Odysseus is known as Ulysses. A great poem of his adventures was called *The Odyssey*, written by Homer in the ninth century B.C.

Following the end of the Trojan War, Odysseus dearly missed his wife, Penelope, and his family. It had been many years since he had seen the land of his birth in the Aegean Sea. Weary and tired from the demands of a long, hard war, Odysseus was looking forward to being reunited with those he loved.

The voyage home, however, was fraught with danger. Odysseus could not foresee the adventures and challenges that he would face. He left the shores of Troy with his men and set sail for Ithaca, expecting a smooth voyage.

Their first stop was the city of the Ciconians, at Ismarus. The inhabitants of this land were not friendly, and killed six of Odysseus's men. Setting out to sea once more, the ship encountered a terrible storm. Odysseus sought refuge in the land of the Lotus-eaters.

Odysseus left the shores of Troy with his men and set sail for Ithaca, expecting a smooth voyage.

Unlike the Ciconians, the Lotus-eaters were friendly people who were only too happy to share their food with the sailors.

When Odysseus's men ate the lotus plants prepared for them, they lost all desire to return to their homes. They became lethargic and content to remain where they were. Odysseus had to drag his men back to his ship in order to continue his voyage.

The ship made its way to the land of the Cyclops, one-eyed giants known for their ferocity and cunning. Despite the danger, Odysseus attempted to disembark on their island in order to gather much needed supplies. With a small band of men, he crept into the cave of Polyphemus, a fearsome, hated Cyclops.

Polyphemus trapped the sailors inside the cave by boarding up the entrance with a giant boulder. Although he had many sheep and cattle to eat, Polyphemus took delight in chasing several sailors through the cave and upon trapping them, killed and ate them.

Odysseus tried to think of a way to escape. He instructed his men to help him sharpen the end of a large log. While the giant slept, Odysseus and several men silently approached Polyphemus and gorged his eye with the point of their crudely made weapon.

Polyphemus cried in pain. Unable to see, he scrambled back and forth in the cave, trying to kill the men who had blinded him. Knowing they could only escape through the entrance to the cave, Polyphemus removed the boulder and stood alongside the opening. He waited patiently for his prey to exit.

Again, Odysseus came up with a clever scheme to trick the Cyclops. He and his men hung onto the bellies of several sheep and goats who were leaving the cave to go to pasture. Even as Polyphemus leaned down to feel the backs of his flock, he was unaware of the secret cargo being carried to freedom. Once outside the cave, Odysseus and his crew boarded their ship.

The Laestrygonians lived near the sea. Their coves and bays were inviting to weary sailors. After many more days at sea, Odysseus saw one of their harbors and instructed his crew to put down an anchor for the evening in order to rest. But that night, under the cover of darkness, the Laestrygonians descended on the ships and destroyed all but the personal ship of Odysseus, which was situated just outside the harbor. Again, Odysseus narrowly escaped harm.

He and his men hung onto the bellies of several sheep and goats who were leaving the cave to go to pasture.

The many perils that Odysseus would face were far from over. When his ship passed the land of the Sirens, sea nymphs who could cast a charm on sailors through their singing, Odysseus gave his men wax plugs to put in their ears. He allowed himself to be tied to the mast of his ship so that he would not be overcome by the irresistible song of the Sirens.

Odysseus had heard of the island of the Thrinacia, where the sun Hyperion kept his flocks of cattle and sheep. Before reaching that place, however, he and his crew would have to pass through the land of the monsters Scylla and Charybdis. Several members of the crew were killed by the six-headed Scylla, who waited patiently on the rocks for her victims. If one was lucky to escape her wrath, Charybdis, the monster of the deep, would create a powerful whirlpool to suck unsuspecting victims into the cold, dark waters of the ocean.

Scylla

With little strength or morale left to them, Odysseus's men made their way to the island of the sun. They dragged their bodies to the shore and surveyed the peaceful lands, where many livestock grazed. Odysseus warned his crew not to kill any of the animals, for they belonged to the god Hyperion. But the temptation for a good meal was too much for the sailors. While Odysseus slept, his men slew several cattle and roasted the meat.

When Odysseus woke, he knew that something terrible had occurred. He urged the crew to board their ship and make way to sail. No sooner had they left the island, when a terrible storm rose from the bottom of the sea, tossing the ship about like a toy. All of the men who had traveled with Odysseus perished. Only he was able to survive by clinging to a piece of the ship's broken mast. Cold and alone in the angry waters, Odysseus drifted far over the waves.

Days passed before Odysseus's body touched dry land. He washed up on the shores of an island that was somehow familiar to him. He was certain that he had seen the trees and fields of this strange place before. But where? Suddenly out of nowhere, a large hound came bounding toward him. Odysseus yelled with joy when he realized that the animal was none other than his faithful dog. At last, he was home!

Odysseus made his way to his palace. His joyous reunion with his wife and son, Telemachus, was short-lived, however, for Odysseus had been absent from Ithaca for over twenty years. Many people were conspiring to take away his throne. No one felt threatened by the strange, old man who had climbed from the sea.

Odysseus challenged the men to an archery contest. One by one, his opponents failed to be as accurate with their bows as the mighty Odysseus. Recognizing the old man for the powerful leader he was, the men declared him king of Ithaca once more. And there, on his beloved island, Odysseus lived out the remainder of his years, delighting his followers with his many tales of adventure.

NATURE

The Laurel of Apollo

The Greek god Zeus was a powerful leader among the gods and goddesses of Olympia. He was feared and respected for his wisdom and his judgment in many situations. Despite his power, Zeus displayed humanlike qualities. He could be quick to anger, fitful, and depressed. He was often passionate, and though he loved his wife Hera very much, he was known to enjoy the company of many beautiful women.

This displeased Hera very much. It caused her to be jealous and bad tempered. When Hera learned that Leto was pregnant with a child of Zeus, she flew into a rage and pursued the poor woman to the four corners of the world. Only on the island of Delos could Leto find a safe haven.

Leto gave birth to twins, Apollo and his sister Artemis. As a sign of joy seven swans circled the area where the children were born. Out of gratitude to the island for granting her asylum from Hera, Leto promised that her son, Apollo, would build a temple there.

Several of the other goddesses did not fear Hera's wrath, and soon descended upon Delos to help Leto with her babies. The goddesses washed the children in sweet water and dressed them in fine clothing. The goddess Themis fed Apollo nectar and ambrosia, which were very special foods reserved for those who were immortal.

Apollo grew into a strong, handsome god. He could play the lyre very well. He was also adept at the art of archery. With his silver bow and arrows, Apollo killed Python, the huge dragon that plagued the inhabitants of Delos.

Apollo traveled to many places. One day, while walking in the Vale (or valley) of Tempe, Apollo saw a beautiful, young maiden partially hidden in a grove of trees. So great was her beauty that Apollo instantly fell in love with her.

The woman's name was Daphne. She had heard many stories of the god Apollo and how well he could shoot a bow and arrow and play the lyre. Daphne was very taken with Apollo's golden, curly hair and clear, blue eyes. She returned his smile.

Apollo

When Apollo tried to approach her, Daphne fled into the woods. This action confused Apollo. Perhaps the young woman was shy, he thought to himself. If only he could talk to her, perhaps she would see that he was a kind and good being who did not wish her harm.

As Daphne ran into the woods, she grew fearful that Apollo would eventually overtake her. She had vowed that no man would ever possess her, not even a god as talented and good as Apollo. She ran harder and harder, trying to elude him.

Daphne knew the valley very well. She ducked into caves and behind great trees to hide from Apollo. But it was of no use. He was determined to speak with her. No matter where she ran, Apollo was able to find her.

Finally Daphne could run no farther. Her legs were tired and her feet ached. There was no place in the woods that she loved where she could hide from the determined Apollo.

Apollo saw that Daphne was growing tired. He called out to her.

"Please don't run from me," he told her. "I do not mean you any harm. I would just like to talk to you."

Daphne could hear Apollo approaching closer and closer to her. When fatigue had completely overtaken her body, she fell to the ground. Desperate and afraid, Daphne cried aloud.

"Mother Earth, please have mercy on me! I have vowed that no man will ever take me. I would rather die than to lose my freedom and my life in these sacred woods. Please, save me!"

The moment Apollo caught up with the breathless Daphne and placed his hands on her shoulders, a very strange thing happened. The beautiful, young woman, who had enchanted the god, began to quiver and shake. Where her body had been, a tall, strong trunk began to grow from the ground. It grew higher and higher, sprouting branches and leaves as it rose upward. Daphne's slender legs descended into the earth, turning into gnarled roots that held fast to the dirt and stones.

Apollo was astonished. He watched in amazement as Daphne became a tree, forever saved from his advances. Apollo realized that despite the fact that he was a god and immortal, his will was no match for Mother Earth's love for her child, Daphne. He watched the sun as it played on the rustling leaves that had once been Daphne's hair. Sadly he reached up and took some leaves from the branches. He wove these into a laurel, which he placed on his head. For the rest of his days, Apollo would wear the laurel to remember Daphne, who chose to remain in the woods she so loved as a beautiful tree.

The Great Warrior Achilles

The Trojan War was one of the most famous events recorded in Greek mythology. Many stories are written of its heroes and heroines, as well as the gods and goddesses who influenced its outcome. Here is the story of the Greek hero Achilles.

The Trojan War began when Helen, the wife of King Menelaus of Sparta, was kidnapped by Paris of Troy. Paris carried Helen far across the Aegean Sea and refused to return her to her husband. For ten years legions and armies of Greece attempted to rescue Helen from Troy.

Achilles was the son of Peleus, a prince, and Thetis, a Nereid, or fairy. It was Thetis's plan to protect her child in a very special way. Since she was immortal, she decided to give her son Achilles some of the supernatural powers that she possessed. Thetis wrapped her baby in a blanket and secretly took him to the underground world of Hades. The river Styx flowed through this dark landscape where the souls of the dead came to rest after their lives on earth were through.

Thetis held her infant son by his tiny, pink heel and dipped him in the powerful waters of the Styx. Little Achilles let out a terrified cry, for the river was bitter cold. But it possessed a remarkable power. Upon contact, the water would form a protective covering over the baby's skin.

Thetis returned from the underworld with Achilles. Not simply content to offer her son the gift of protective armor, she vowed that she would also make him immortal. Thetis prepared a large fire. She held Achilles over it. When she was about to immerse his tiny body in the flames, her husband, Peleus, came upon her. Thinking that she was trying to harm Achilles, Peleus pushed her away from the fire. Thetis fled with Achilles.

Thetis gave Achilles to the care of Chiron, a wise centaur who had been the tutor of many Greek heroes. Achilles grew into a capable and strong, young man. When the Trojan War broke out, he was eager to go and fight for the honor of Helen. He wished to fight under the command of General Agamemnon.

When Thetis heard of her son's plans, she implored Chiron to convince him not to go to war. But Chiron would not persuade Achilles to forget about fighting. He knew that Achilles had the makings of a great warrior.

In desperation Thetis placed a spell on her son, rendering him powerless. Then she disguised him as a young girl and sent him away to the island of Scyros, where he would be under the protection of King Lycomedes.

Meanwhile, Agamemnon gathered his troops for the siege of Troy. His men were strong and willing to fight. Victory seemed certain. A seer by the name of Calchas, however, predicted that the Greeks would not win the war unless a warrior named Achilles was on their side.

Hearing a rumor that such a man was living on the island of Scyros, Agamemnon dispatched several men to find him. Among them was Odysseus.

Odysseus offered many fine gifts to the daughters of King Lycomedes. He placed precious jewels and fine cloth before them. All but one daughter was enchanted by Odysseus's gifts. When Odysseus withdrew a spectacular sword from his belt and placed it in front of the young women, he immediately recognized a glint of delight in the eyes of the daughter who was not impressed with his other gifts. The young girl seized the sword.

"You are Achilles!" Odysseus declared. "You can no longer live here under the protection of your mother, who would have you be a girl. You are destined to be a great fighter on the side of Agamemnon!"

Achilles departed with Odysseus and entered the battlefield of Troy. He fought bravely and ferociously with his fellow Greeks, who greatly admired his skills. Achilles even slew Hector, the son of the Trojan king, Priam.

Weary of all the fighting, and respectful of Achilles's kindness in allowing him to reclaim the body of his dead son, King Priam declared a truce. Unfortunately, Paris was afraid that he would have to return Helen to her husband. He did not want to see the war come to an end. From a tower high atop Priam's palace, Paris shot an arrow at Achilles.

The arrow pierced Achilles in the back of his foot. This was the only spot where the magical river Styx had not touched his body, because his mother had held him by his heel when she dipped him in its water. Soon after being injured, Achilles died.

The death of the great warrior inspired Agamemnon and Odysseus to continue to fight. After many battles and many deaths, the Greeks succeeded in defeating the Trojans and rescuing Helen. The exploits of Achilles in the Trojan War were recorded in *The Iliad*, the famous poem by Homer, which is still enjoyed by readers to this day.

Aphrodite, Goddess of Love

Many of the Greek goddesses were well-known for their physical beauty. One was Aphrodite, the goddess of love. She was the subject of many paintings and sculptures throughout history. In Roman mythology she was called Venus.

Aphrodite means "she who was raised from the foam," since the ancient Greeks believed that the goddess appeared out of the ocean waves. She was brought ashore on the island of Cyprus, where she was dressed in finery by the daughters of the goddess Themis.

Aphrodite possessed a magic girdle that had the power to attract any man she desired. With her girdle and matchless beauty, the goddess succeeded in causing much trouble. Many men fell in love with her. The more people praised her good looks, the more vain and powerful she grew. She was not well liked by the other Greek goddesses.

One day Aphrodite wished to conduct a contest to see who among the goddesses was the most beautiful. Hera, the wife of the god Zeus, and Athena, Zeus's daughter, were the other contestants. They chose Paris, the prince of Troy, to be the judge.

The contest was to have dire consequences for everyone. Paris was instructed to give a golden apple to the most beautiful of the three women. He thought carefully about his decision. Hera was indeed quite influential because of her husband. Athena was as wise as she was attractive. And there was no question that Aphrodite possessed incredible beauty. Whom would Paris choose?

In the end he handed the golden apple to Aphrodite. As a reward for choosing her, Aphrodite assisted Paris in kidnapping Helen, the wife of a Greek king. This incident was the cause of the long, terrible Trojan War, in which the Greeks and Trojans fought for ten years.

It was not the only problem that Aphrodite would cause. She forced Eos, the dawn, to fall hopelessly in love with Orion. When she learned that the women of Lemnos would not worship her as a goddess, she placed a terrible curse upon them. They were plagued with a horrible odor that made them undesirable to their husbands. Aphrodite's mischief was legendary.

Although Aphrodite was promised in marriage to the crippled, deformed god Hephaestus, she did not love him and continued to pursue and attract many other gods and men. Poseidon, the god of the sea, tried to win her love. So did Hermes, the messenger god who promised to take her in his chariot around the universe. Even the handsome Apollo, with his talents in music and the arts, attempted to win her for his own. Aphrodite, however, desired none of these gods.

Hephaestus was aware of his wife's behavior. Her attitude toward other men displeased him. He knew he could not persuade the beautiful Aphrodite to be faithful to him alone. He was a short, ugly man with gnarled arms and twisted legs. So he devised a plan to embarrass his wife in front of all the other gods and goddesses of the kingdom of Olympus.

One evening when Hephaestus knew that Aphrodite would visit her latest admirer, Ares, the Greek god of war, he entered their meeting place before they arrived and constructed a special net that would fall down upon the two lovers and trap them. Just as the jealous Hephaestus had planned, Ares and Aphrodite were entangled in the net, unable to escape. The other gods and goddesses came to look at them and ridicule them. This upset Ares very much. He was a great warrior and very proud. He offered to pay a heavy compensation to Hephaestus in return for releasing him from the net. Believing that justice had been served, Hephaestus did just that.

Aphrodite means "she who was raised from the foam."

Aphrodite was also embarrassed by her husband's trick. She did not remain angry for long, however. After a short period of time, she was flaunting her beauty in front of everyone, as if nothing had happened.

Of all the men Aphrodite admired, Adonis was her favorite. He was a child when she first saw him. Moved by his beauty, Aphrodite gave him to Persephone, the queen of the underworld, to raise. Persephone's affection for the child grew every day. When Aphrodite returned to claim Adonis, who was now a handsome young man, Persephone refused to give him up. The two goddesses quarreled.

Aphrodite and Adonis

The god Zeus was asked to decide who should have Adonis. In hopes of not upsetting either goddess, Zeus decided to allow Adonis to remain on his own for one-third of the year, then stay with Aphrodite for one-third of the year, and Persephone for the remainder of the year. This arrangement seemed to please the two women. However, their happiness would be short-lived.

One day while hunting, young Adonis was attacked by a wild boar. Aphrodite ran to his aid, but she arrived too late to save him. As she hurried to his side, she scratched her foot on a rose bush. Out of respect for her grief for the dying Adonis, the roses on the bush turned from white to crimson red. To this day, throughout Greece, the flowers are a reminder of Aphrodite's great affection for the handsome Adonis.

FIRE AND LIGHTNING

The Flight of Daedalus and Icarus

Daedalus was a master craftsman who lived in Athens. He was known for his talents in architecture and the fine arts. Everyone who saw his work praised him.

Daedalus was also a fine inventor. He invented the chisel and the ax for cutting and shaping wood. He devised the first sails for ships, thus harnessing the power of the winds to move people on the oceans.

Many men worked for Daedalus in his workshop in Athens. It was an honor to be his apprentice. Even his own nephew Talus came to work with him and learn from his skill. Daedalus was only too pleased to share his knowledge with the young people who were eager to work for him. But when he saw just how talented Talus was, and how he drew the attention of his fellow students, Daedalus became jealous.

One day Talus was working on an assignment at the Acropolis in Athens. The Acropolis was an immense temple, built high atop a cliff. As night fell, all of the young workers returned to the workshop, except for Talus. When his absence was noticed, the townspeople began to become suspicious. What had happened to the young boy who had so obviously inherited his uncle's gift of craftsmanship?

Daedalus offered a feeble explanation for Talus's disappearance. He told a court of inquiry that his nephew must have fallen from one of the cliffs of the Acropolis into the sea. The explanation seemed feasible because Talus's body was never recovered. It did not convince the court, however, and Daedalus was banished from the city of Athens. No one knew for certain if he was guilty or not.

Daedalus and his only son, Icarus, traveled to the kingdom of Crete at the invitation of its king, Minos. King Minos knew of Daedalus's reputation as an artist and builder and hoped to use his skills. Daedalus and Icarus agreed to work for Minos.

King Minos demanded a tribute from each of the cities under his rule. Every year seven young men and seven young women were offered as a sacrifice to the Minotaur, a man-eating bull who lived in a maze called the Labyrinth of Cnossus. The maze had been designed by Daedalus for King Minos a long time ago.

One year Daedalus's cousin Theseus was chosen for the sacrifice. When Theseus arrived in Crete with the other victims, King Minos's daughter Adriane saw him and instantly fell in love with him. She could not bear the thought of him being eaten by the horrible Minotaur.

Adriane knew that Theseus and Daedalus were relatives. She knew that Daedalus had created the maze. She appealed to Daedalus to help her save Theseus's life. At first Daedalus refused. He was afraid to go against the wishes of King Minos. After a time, however, he was moved by the pleas of Adriane for the life of his cousin. He confided to her the way in which to slaughter the bull. First he made her swear that she would never divulge the information that he gave her.

Daedalus told Adriane that the bull could be killed if he was stabbed by one of his own horns. Adriane passed the secret to Theseus, who was about to enter the maze.

Once inside, Theseus faced the Minotaur. Its fearsome image caused him to tremble in fear, but he did not forget the instructions that had been passed to him. He waited for the beast to charge him, then grabbed one of its curved horns and snapped it from its head. Before the startled beast could recover from its shock, Theseus thrust the sharp horn into its head, killing it.

Theseus then ran from the maze. He escaped from the island of Crete with Adriane at his side. When King Minos found out what had happened, he was enraged. He knew that Daedalus was the only person who could possibly possess the secrets of the Labyrinth of Cnossus. Thus, he imprisoned Daedalus and Icarus in a tower.

The two men were resigned to live the remainder of their lives in the lonely solitude of the tower cell. After all, they reasoned, they had each other's company. Soon, though, that would not be enough. Daedalus began to scheme of ways to escape from the clutches of King Minos.

Using his extraordinary skills, Daedalus constructed a set of wings for himself and his son. He built them from scraps of wood tied together with strings. He plucked the feathers from two eagles that he had lured to the tower window, and fastened the feathers to the wooden frames with wax. Then he built harnesses for each pair of wings.

Daedalus and Icarus

Daedalus instructed Icarus to wear the wings.

"Follow me," he told his son. "Be certain not to fly too low, or you may crash into the ocean. Also, be careful not to fly too close to the sun, or the wax will melt from your wings and you will fall from the sky."

Icarus excitedly strapped on his wings and jumped from the tower window after his father. Together they soared over the island of Crete until they saw the vast ocean below them.

The feel of the wind on his face was very exhilarating for Icarus. After so many months of exile in the tower of King Minos, he was at last free! Filled with a sense of joy, he rose on the strong currents of wind. Higher and higher he climbed into the air, piercing the very clouds with his great golden wings.

Together they soared over the island of Crete until they saw the vast ocean below them.

The feathers began to fall from his wings at an alarming rate.

Icarus soon forgot his father's warning. Losing all sense of logic, he flew toward the great orb of the sun. The air grew hotter and hotter as he rose upward. To his dismay, Icarus noticed that it was becoming more difficult to fly. He glanced over his shoulder and looked at his wings. One by one they were losing the eagles' feathers as the sun melted the wax that held them to the wooden frame.

Icarus attempted to escape from the sun's heat by gliding lower toward the earth. But it was too late. The feathers began to fall from his wings at an alarming rate. Daedalus watched in horror as his son began to panic. Icarus tumbled toward the earth.

"Save me, Father!" he called to Daedalus.

Daedalus tried to reach him in vain. The young man plunged into the sea. With tears in his eyes and a heavy heart, Daedalus continued on his sad journey. He could not believe that fate would exact such a heavy price for his own freedom. Even to this very day, the water where his beloved son fell is called the Icarian Sea.

The Wooden Horse of Troy

Early one morning when the fog had not yet lifted from the walled city of Troy, a sleepy guard looked over the great gates of the town and spied a terrifying sight.

A massive wooden horse, nearly as tall as the gates themselves, was positioned outside. Its cold stare and enormous size frightened the guard, who picked up his horn with trembling hands and sounded a warning.

Troy had been under attack by the Greeks for many years. The Greek army had sailed across the sea from their homeland to fight a battle in retaliation for the kidnapping of the Greek queen Helen, by Paris, the prince of Troy.

Stirred by the sound of the guard's horn, the people of Troy woke from their beds. They were always prepared for an attack by the armies of Greece. Today was no different from any other day. They scrambled for safety inside their homes. The men of the Trojan army quickly found their weapons.

The guard called to the people, "Behold a strange object that is left outside our gates!"

When the people heard him, they shook their heads in wonder. What sort of joke was this? They hurried to the top of the high walls and looked down to where the guard was pointing.

To their amazement they saw a replica of a soldier's steed constructed of wood. It was perched on a large wooden platform with wheels. No one spoke.

Cautiously several soldiers climbed down off the walls and approached the statue. A small plaque on its side read, "In honor of Athena."

The Trojans were confused. As far as they could see, in every direction there was a calmness and tranquillity to the landscape that they had not experienced in years. There were no Greek soldiers to be seen; no smoking camp fires, no calls to arms or battle cries.

Inspecting the giant horse from every angle, the soldiers could find nothing unusual on its surface. They prodded and poked it with their spears. They tapped on its hooves. They clambered upon its back, examining its thick neck and stiff mane. Its glass eyes gave no indication of danger. The wooden steed was silent and still in the morning air.

A soldier suggested that the horse was a request for peace from the Greek army, and that the people of Troy should consent to bring it within the gates of the city. The people argued back and forth. Could it be true that the Greeks desired peace after so long and terrible a battle? Finally all agreed to allow the horse to be brought inside, since it was a tribute to the great goddess Athena and appeared to be harmless. Tying a rope to its neck, the soldiers pulled the horse on wheels through the gates of Troy. They displayed it in the city's center. Then the soldiers closed the gates again, still slightly baffled at the unexpected gift left outside their city that morning.

In the evening the Trojans gathered once again around the base of the wooden horse. They lit bonfires and offered tributes to the goddess Athena. They played musical instruments and danced. A great feast was held with food enough for the entire army and townspeople. Vats of wine were opened, and everyone drank and sang. The Trojans were eager for peace and eager for the opportunity to celebrate and be joyful.

After several hours passed, the people began to get tired. They collapsed from drinking too much wine and from dancing too long and hard. They were soon gathered in heaps, here and there, all over the city. The moon rose high in the sky, and the stars shone down on the sleeping revelers of Troy.

As they slumbered, a small wooden panel slid open beneath the belly of the horse. One by one, a group of armed men jumped down onto the platform and crept among

With swords drawn and ready to fight, a fierce contingent of Greek soldiers had stolen into the heart of Troy, undetected.

the sleeping people. With swords drawn and ready to fight, a fierce contingent of Greek soldiers had stolen into the heart of Troy undetected.

Horrified, the Trojans woke up from their feast to find themselves under siege. They scrambled to find their weapons, but it was too late. The Greek army clearly had an advantage. They opened the once-protective gates of Troy and allowed their fellow soldiers to enter. They began to slay the Trojans without mercy. Even the city's army could not organize itself in time to defend the people.

When the surprise attack was over, hundreds of Trojan soldiers lay dead within the walls of the great city. Women and children were taken as prisoners of the cunning Greek army. Helen was rescued from her captors and returned to her husband.

To this day the phrase "Trojan Horse" still refers to a suspicious gift that is given to someone in order to trick them.

Hermes, Messenger of the Gods

Today it is easy to send messages around the world. We have electronic mail through our computers, telephones, fax machines, and delivery services like those of the Post Office. In ancient times, however, messages were conveyed in a different way. They were delivered by heralds, or messengers, people who were hired or appointed to bring special news from one person to another.

Imagine a man dressed in white with a round hat on top of his head. In his hand he carries a staff with white ribbons, and on his feet he wears a pair of sandals with golden wings. This was the messenger Hermes, who was appointed by Zeus, the most powerful god of Greek mythology.

Zeus did not choose Hermes because of his speed or agility. He chose him because Hermes was a clever individual—capable of tricking people in a playful sense. He earned Zeus's admiration through a series of events that unfolded when he was very young.

Hermes was the son of Zeus and Maia, the daughter of Atlas. He was born in a cave on Mount Cyllene in Arcadia. Hermes was anything but an ordinary immortal baby! He was extremely inquisitive and wished to know everything about the world firsthand. Though Maia had wrapped him tightly in a blanket and placed him in his cradle for safekeeping, Hermes managed to escape—undetected by his mother—and set out for adventure.

Descending down the mountain, Hermes saw a herd of white cows. He wanted to have some fun. He decided to play a trick on the owner of the animals. Hermes herded the cows into a pen and covered their hooves with long reed grass that he had gathered from the riverbed. Then he led the cows to a deep ravine, where it would be difficult to find them. With their hooves covered with reeds, no one would be able to tell from what direction they had come.

The herd of white cows belonged to the god Apollo. When he discovered that they were missing, he searched for them throughout the countryside. After several days of searching, he came to a cave. Apollo heard the sound of beautiful music coming from the mouth of the cave and decided to investigate. He found the young Hermes playing a crude instrument made from a tortoiseshell.

"Where did you get that musical instrument?" Apollo asked the young boy.

"I made it!" Hermes declared proudly. "I used the shell of a tortoise and the dried intestines of a white cow for strings. I call it a lyre."

Apollo hesitated for a moment. "The intestines of a white cow? You didn't happen to come upon my white cows, did you?"

Hermes was surprised by Apollo's question. He had no idea that the cows belonged to the god.

"I'm sorry," he said, "I didn't know they were yours. I'll lead you to them right away!"

Apollo pretended to be mad at the young boy, but in reality he was quite amused by the child's inventiveness and bravery.

He decided to take Hermes with him to Olympus. Perhaps the god Zeus would enjoy the story of what his son Hermes had done.

Indeed, Zeus was amused by the tale. He found Hermes clever and playful. He admired his sense of adventure. Zeus asked Hermes to be his messenger.

"By this post you will deliver my word to all the gods and goddesses on my behalf. You will protect travelers and merchants." Then the great god smiled as he added, "I hope you will not be too mischievous in your job."

Indeed, Hermes did his job well. Zeus provided him with a special staff that would announce that he was the messenger of Olympus. He also gave him swift sandals for his feet, with a pair of powerful wings attached to each one.

Hermes

Among his responsibilities, Hermes was in charge of guiding the souls of the dead to the underworld kingdom of Hades. He brought them to the dark land beneath the world, to the banks of the river Styx, where the ferryman Charon would conduct them across the water to their final resting place.

Hermes was also famous for many other things. Not only had he invented the first lyre, but he discovered how to make a fire from dried kindling. He devised a method for measuring and weighing grain. He is credited with creating the alphabet for writing words, as well as a system for studying the stars. He even became the patron of the art of wrestling, for it was said that he brought good luck wherever he traveled.

Throughout his career, however, he still enjoyed a bit of fun whenever he could. With his winning ways and carefully constructed arguments, Hermes found it easy to trick people, though he always told the truth and delivered Zeus's messages in a timely manner.

Life After Death: The Underworld

Death was not the end of one's existence, according to the ancient Greeks. They believed that when people died, their souls traveled to the underworld. The underworld was not necessarily a place of punishment where the dead were sent to atone for their sins. Rather, it was a final destination for the souls of mortals and immortals alike. Some souls were punished in the underworld, such as those who had displeased or insulted the gods and goddesses during their lives on earth.

There are countless stories in Greek mythology involving the underworld. One of the most famous stories is that of Demeter and Persephone. Demeter was the Greek goddess of agriculture and the harvest. No doubt, she was a very important deity. When her only daughter, Persephone, was abducted by Hades, the king of the underworld, Demeter was filled with grief and sorrow. She withheld her blessing from the earth, and consequently, no crops grew. Finally the great god Zeus intervened in the quest to rescue Persephone by asking Hades to release her to her mother for part of the year. Thus, Persephone remained with Hades to be his queen, except in springtime when she would return to Demeter. This myth helps to explain the seasons of the year. Whenever Persephone was

Hades

reunited with Demeter, the earth experienced springtime and became green and fertile again. As soon as she took her place on the throne next to her husband, Hades, the world experienced winter and became cold and barren.

To reach Hades's kingdom, the souls of the dead would travel to the river Styx. This river was one of several rivers that flowed through the underworld. The others were known as Acheron, or the river of pain; Cocytus, the river of groans; Phlegethon, the river of fire; and Lethe, the river of forgetfulness. Once on the shores of the Styx, the dead would wait to be ushered into the underworld by the ferryman Charon. Charon was an old, withered man, who piloted his barge with great seriousness. Charon would only accept the souls of those who had been properly buried. He would ask for the fee of an obolos, or penny, for the journey. If people had not been buried with the proper rites, or could not pay for the ferry crossing, they were doomed to wander along the riverbanks for one hundred years.

Charon's barge would float on the Styx until it arrived at the entrance to Hades's kingdom. Along the way the souls of the dead would witness many frightening sights. Monsters and beasts, like the Hydra and Chimera, would pose on the riverbanks. The three Furies—Tisiphone, Alecto, and Megaera—might make an appearance to the newly dead. One might also get a glimpse of the hounds of hell, or the Keres, which were fierce canines that pursued those souls who had committed crimes and attempted to escape punishment. It was the responsibility of the Furies to intervene in disputes between mortals and to settle the affairs justly. Thus, they were a powerfully respected trio, even though their black deformed bodies bore bats' wings, and they possessed wriggling snakes for hair.

Charon delivered his charges to the great gates, the entrance to the kingdom of Hades and Persephone. These grotesque, twisted gates were guarded by Cerberus, a dog with three heads and three serpents' tails. Cerberus made certain that only the dead entered Hades. No living person was allowed in, although there are a few stories of individuals who convinced Charon and Cerberus to allow them to pass through the gates.

Certain souls were judged for their behavior on earth. They were brought before a council of the three judges: Minos, Aeacus, and Rhadamanthus. If the dead souls had angered the gods or goddesses during their lifetime, they were sent to an area in Hades known as Tartarus. It was in Tartarus that the gods had their vengeance on the poor unfortunates who had crossed them. Tityus, the giant who had attacked the mother of the god Apollo, was chained and tortured there, as well as Ixion from the kingdom of Thessaly, who had dared to flirt with Zeus's wife Hera.

The souls of those who had lived valiant lives were sometimes sent to the glorious Elysian Fields. Here, they were allowed to exist in harmony and peace, honored for their actions in battle. The many soldiers who had fought during the Trojan War were ushered to the Elysian Fields, where they were rewarded with blue skies, sunshine, ample food, entertainment, and beautiful meadows in which they could wander and roam.

It was unusual for a soul to appear directly before the king of the underworld, Hades. Occasionally a petition, or request for mercy, was brought to Hades's queen, Persephone. She was well-known for her compassionate ways and her ability to convince Hades to intervene on behalf of a troubled soul.

Thus, the world that followed death was as important to the ancient Greeks as the realms of the earth, sea, and sky. The many colorful personalities who dwelled there, and the souls of those who were carried there, are the subjects of many fantastic stories, which are told to this day.

IMMORTALITY

The Family of Gods at Olympus

The ancient Greeks worshipped a family of gods who ruled the universe. The gods lived atop Mount Olympus in northern Greece. It was believed to be the highest point in the world.

Olympus was truly a paradise. It was never cold there. It never rained. Fragrant flowers grew everywhere, and the strains of beautiful music filled the air, day and night. The entrance to Olympus was a "gate of clouds," which was tended to by the goddesses of the seasons. The gates opened to allow the gods and goddesses to journey to earth and return to Olympus.

Of the gods who dwelled on Olympus, no one was more powerful than Zeus. He lived in a magnificent palace where all the other gods gathered at his request. In his great hall the gods feasted on nectar and ambrosia, a delicious food that was only eaten by those who were immortal.

Zeus's architects created magnificent buildings as dwellings for the gods. Golden shoes for the gods and goddesses were fashioned by Zeus's smiths. Even the horses that pulled the chariots of Olympus were shod in brass shoes that gleamed as they trotted along the streets.

The gods were dressed splendidly in gold and silver robes. They lived in their own palaces, surrounded by magical gardens and streams. The gods liked to travel to earth and become involved in the lives of humans. Occasionally they protected people from danger or misfortune.

Among the most powerful gods that surrounded Zeus were Poseidon, god of the sea; Hephaestus, the smith; Ares, the god of war; Hermes, the messenger of Zeus; and Apollo, the god of music. Athena, goddess of wisdom, and Hera, Zeus's wife, also lived there along with Aphrodite, the goddess of love; Artemis, the goddess of the hunt; Hestia, the goddess of the home; and Demeter, the goddess of agriculture.

There were also lesser gods who gathered in Olympus at the request of Zeus, such as Hades, god of the underworld, and Pan, a goat-horned, goat-legged god of the countryside.

Where did these powerful gods come from?

It was believed that at one time the universe was in a state of chaos, or confusion. From this state, Mother Earth appeared. She had a consort, or mate, Uranus, who created everything in the universe.

With Uranus, Mother Earth bore twelve children known as the "Titans." Of these children, the youngest son, Cronus, became a leader in an uprising against his own father, Uranus.

Cronus took Rhea as his wife. He feared that their children would one day overthrow him as he had done to his father. To prevent this, Cronus swallowed each of his children after they were born. Rhea managed to save one child from Cronus's horrible actions. She took her baby Zeus to Mount Lycaeum and hid him in a cave.

Cronus became suspicious. He searched for Rhea's child. Zeus was moved from place to place to save his life. Finally, Rhea decided to wrap a heavy stone in a blanket and present it to Cronus as her baby. Cronus, thinking that he had found Rhea's child, swallowed the stone and was convinced that he was safe from the threat of an uprising by his offspring.

Zeus grew into a powerful god. He was the god of the sky, the thunder, and the rain. He became known as the first of a race of new gods. Zeus took Hera as his wife, and together they had many children. Zeus also had many children with other wives. His children included the gods and goddesses who lived with him in Olympus.

Despite his wisdom, Zeus often fell prey to jealousy and fits of rage. He tried to keep his children in line and often quarreled with Hera. Zeus enjoyed the company of beautiful women, and this angered Hera. He enjoyed teasing Hera. Once he created a statue of a woman that he placed in his chariot as he drove through the streets of Olympus.

Thinking that her husband was being unkind to her, Hera stopped the chariot and threw herself at the woman she believed to be Zeus's latest love. How foolish Hera felt when she discovered that the woman was made of stone!

When humans became greedy and selfish, Zeus decided to flood the earth and create a new race of people. From his throne on Mount Olympus, Zeus ruled the universe with passion and anger, delight and concern. Many myths tell of the colorful deeds and enormous power of the father of the Greek gods.

Monsters of Greek Mythology

Imagine that you are invited to visit the Greek gods and goddesses at their home high atop Mount Olympus. You find everything in this special world exciting and breathtaking. The music playing lightly in the air is the sweetest you have heard. The food is so satisfying and so delicious that you can't wait for the next course to arrive from the kitchens. Sweet nectar is poured from bejeweled chalices. There are overstuffed chairs and stools for you to sit on and rest your feet.

As you walk along the streets of Olympus, admiring the spectacular architecture and fragrant gardens, suddenly someone taps you on the shoulder. You turn to face a young man who asks you for directions. Glancing down at his feet, you notice that he is walking on hooves! Although he is a man from the waist up—his lower body is that of a horse! You have come in contact with a centaur—a creature who is half human, half horse.

If Olympus had a zoo, it would be filled with other amazing beings, as well. There would be sea nymphs and wood nymphs, fairies and ogres, great horned monsters and tiny elves.

Perhaps you would find yourself staring at Cerberus, the three-headed dog who guards the gates of the dark underworld. Next to him would be the fascinating and frightening Chimera—a beast who is half goat and half lion, with the tail of a powerful viper. Above you the silent air is disturbed by the thrashing of mighty wings. It is only Pegasus, the flying horse.

He warns you to take care not to stand too close to the Hydra, a beast with thousands and thousands of deadly snakes writhing from its hair. Then he flies high in the sky to pursue the Harpies, birdlike creatures who possess the faces of ugly, old women. The Harpies enjoy stealing food from people and tormenting them. They scatter, however, when they see Pegasus coming for them.

The beasts and monsters of Greek mythology had many powers. Though they were not as powerful as the gods and goddesses who dwelled on Olympus, they could definitely disturb the plans and actions of the gods and mortals.

Among the monsters you might encounter would be the Gorgons. These were three-headed females with huge razor-sharp teeth, needlelike claws, and snakes for hair. If someone dared to look directly at them, they turned the unfortunate observer into stone. Most famous of the Gorgons was Medusa, who had once been a beautiful woman. From her severed head the swift Pegasus was born.

Medusa

When humans could not find a suitable solution to a problem, they might call upon the avenging Furies, who lived in the underworld of Hades. Alecto, Megaera, and Tisiphone would often achieve justice in a difficult situation. The Furies looked like black dogs with bats' wings. They carried whips, which they used when someone broke the law.

Above you the silent air is disturbed by the thrashing of mighty wings. It is only Pegasus, the flying horse.

High atop the mountains of ancient Greece, one might stumble upon the gigantic nests of creatures called Griffins. The Griffin was a monster with the body of a lion and the head and wings of an eagle. Its back was covered with long feathers. Since Griffins liked to build their nests near deposits of gold, they were often followed and hunted by plunderers and thieves. It was not easy for them to hide their rooks from the greedy.

Near the source of the great Nile River lived a nation of very small people known as Pygmies. A Pygmy was only thirteen inches tall. Though they were small in stature, the Pygmies were fierce warriors. They even did battle with the Greek hero Heracles. They did not win, however, for Heracles managed to subdue them by entrapping them in a lion's skin.

The Sphinx is certainly one of the most famous monsters in Greek mythology. With the body of a lioness and the upper torso of a woman, the Sphinx would lie quietly in the sand, waiting for her next victim. It was customary for her to pose a riddle to whoever happened to venture too near to her. The clever Sphinx often outwitted those she challenged. According to legend she was unable to trick a man called Oedipus who happened to come upon her one day.

The Sphinx asked Oedipus if he knew what thing walked on four feet in the morning, two feet in the afternoon, and three feet in the evening. Oedipus looked around him at the skeletons of those who had not guessed correctly the answer to the riddle. He thought for a moment, then responded to the great beast.

"It is man who first crawls on his hands and legs when he is a baby. When he is grown, he walks on two feet. But in his old age he may have need of a cane or walking stick, and so walks on 'three legs.'"

The Sphinx had no choice but to let the clever Oedipus continue on his way, for he had answered her riddle.

Be certain not to wander into the land of the Sphinx unless you are prepared to take up her challenge. Then, you can only hope that the winged horse Pegasus will be prepared to swoop down and rescue you if you happen to answer incorrectly!

Orpheus in the Land of the Dead

Orpheus, son of the god Apollo, loved to play his lyre, a small, stringed instrument that resembled a harp. The strains of his beautiful music enchanted both gods and mortals. It calmed the wild beasts and birds. Even the streams and rocks absorbed the wonderful noise like warm sunshine.

Apollo blessed the marriage of his son to the lovely wood nymph, Eurydice. Although Eurydice and Orpheus were very much in love, Eurydice occasionally grew weary of the great palace in which they lived. She longed for the fragrant fields and woodlands of her home.

One day, while playing with her sister nymphs in a grove of trees, Eurydice was spotted by the god of the hunt, Aristaeus. Upon seeing the beautiful woman, Aristaeus dropped his bow and arrow, forgetting all about the agile deer he was pursuing.

"You are every bit as wondrous as I was told!" Aristaeus declared to Eurydice.

Eurydice was startled by the handsome god, who had appeared suddenly in the woods. She blushed.

"Please, sir," she responded. "I am not flattered by your speech. Be on your way."

Orpheus

Aristaeus could not believe his ears. "You dare speak that way to a god?"

"Sir," Eurydice said matter-of-factly, "you may be a god, but my husband is Orpheus, son of Apollo. He would not be pleased by your lack of manners."

Aristaeus laughed. "I am not afraid of Orpheus, who loves music above all things." He moved toward Eurydice.

Frightened by his boldness, Eurydice fled into the woods. She ran as fast as her nimble legs could carry her. But it was difficult to elude Aristaeus, who was used to chasing prey through the thick underbrush.

Eurydice looked for a place to hide. She climbed a rocky slope and jumped down into a clearing, alarming many birds, which quickly took to flight. She did not look back at the figure of Aristaeus. Finally, overcome with fatigue, Eurydice slowed down long enough to realize that the god of the hunt was no longer pursuing her.

She fell into a heap on the ground. In no time her eyes closed with sleep.

Eurydice did not see the tiny viper that crawled among the surrounding rocks. She did not feel his bite on her bared leg. Within minutes the viper's deadly poison spread through Eurydice's body.

Orpheus was concerned when his wife did not return from the fields. He paced through the great halls of his palace. Finally, he commanded several servants to comb the countryside in search of her.

With terrible sadness the servants returned the body of Eurydice to Orpheus. The sight of his dead wife caused Orpheus to become filled with inconsolable grief. Nothing could calm him. Day after day he played sad songs on his lyre inside the palace walls. He would not eat, nor could he sleep.

"I must go to the underworld and retrieve my one true love," Orpheus declared to his father.

Apollo was greatly distressed at his son's reaction. "Don't be foolish, Orpheus," he told him. "You cannot undo what has been done. Leave Eurydice to the land of the dead."

But Orpheus did not listen to his father's counsel. Taking his lyre, he left his comfortable palace and began the long journey to Hades, the underworld. Near the Ionian Sea, Orpheus found a deep chasm that led him to the river Styx. It was here that he found the ferryman Charon, who carried the dead across the river to the land of Hades.

Charon refused his services to Orpheus. "I can only carry the dead," he told him.

But Orpheus was not discouraged from his quest. Fueled by his longing for his wife, Orpheus began to play sweet songs on his lyre. So touching were the songs he played, that neither Charon nor the creatures that dwelled in the land of darkness could resist their effect.

Orpheus boarded Charon's ferry to the throne of Persephone, queen of the underworld. Even she was moved by the notes that danced from his lyre.

"Please return my wife to me," Orpheus begged Persephone. "I cannot imagine life without her."

Persephone thought of the consequences of such a bold move. Finally she gave in.

"Take Eurydice back with you to the land of the living," she told Orpheus. "But remember my warning to you. If during your ascent to the land of light you turn around and look at your wife, she will be forced to return to Hades."

From the shadows of hell, Eurydice was reunited with Orpheus. She held him to her and was filled with joy.

"Follow me back to our home," Orpheus instructed her.

The two began the long climb to their home. Eurydice could not climb as quickly as Orpheus. She struggled to keep up with him.

Near the opening that led from Hades to the world of the living, Orpheus was overcome by feelings of great joy and accomplishment. He had managed to rescue his beloved wife from the jaws of death. He felt the faint touch of sunlight on his skin and the promise of their life together.

When he turned to encourage Eurydice to come quickly to the light,
Orpheus realized what he had done.

In his excitement Orpheus reached back behind him for Eurydice's hand. "Look, look!" he exclaimed to her. "We are almost there!"

But when he turned to encourage Eurydice to come quickly to the light, Orpheus realized what he had done. The figure of Eurydice, slightly behind him, turned to a pale shadow. She fell back into the horrible chasm, which cut sharply into the earth, until he could no longer see her.

Orpheus raced after the vision of Eurydice. When he again reached the shores of the river Styx, he told Charon what had occurred. But this time Charon was not moved by his story. He refused to bring Orpheus a second time to Hades. Heartbroken, Orpheus exited the underworld without his wife.

Prometheus's Gift to HumanKind

The Greek god Prometheus looked down at the earth from the world of the gods on Mount Olympus. He pitied the humans that lived below.

When the strong gusts of winter winds blew across the mountains and seas of the earth, the people had no fires to warm them. They ate their food cold and uncooked. There were no flames to help them to shape metal into weapons for defense, or tools to assist with harvesting grain. The human race was in need of fire, and Prometheus knew that the most powerful god in the universe, Zeus, had no plan to share this element with the mortals he had created.

Zeus feared that one day human beings would rise like disobedient children against the gods. Zeus behaved like a jealous, strict parent who demanded loyalty from his offspring—in this case, the human race.

Prometheus, however, did not agree with Zeus's treatment of humans. He believed that they could be guided with love and affection to do the right thing. He appealed to Zeus to share the gift of fire with the mortals on earth. Zeus refused to listen.

"Suppose I share fire with them, and they rebel against me?" Zeus asked Prometheus.

"With fire they could eat well, keep warm, and create powerful weapons. Why would they continue to obey me?"

"I believe you can trust them," Prometheus answered. "If they are treated with respect and kindness, they will return it to you."

"I cannot do that. Do not share the power of fire with humans," Zeus warned.

Prometheus found it difficult to obey Zeus's command. During the many festivals that were celebrated on earth, the people were required to share the best selection of meat and other foods with the gods. Prometheus secretly taught them how to disguise their offerings by wrapping bones and fat in the hides of animals so it would appear that they were giving a true sacrifice to the immortals of Mount Olympus.

Zeus eventually discovered what Prometheus was doing. He attempted to keep his anger to himself.

Not content to leave well enough alone, Prometheus thought long and hard about the humans' need for fire. Eventually his compassion for the people of earth won out. He dared to disobey the all-powerful Zeus.

On a dark evening Prometheus ventured to the part of Mount Olympus where the orange, red, and golden flames of eternal fire were dancing on the mountaintop. Unnoticed by the other gods, Prometheus took an ember of the precious fire from the flame and hid it in a stalk of fennel, which is an herb. He hid the ember in his cloak. As he stole away from the home of the gods, he could feel the heat of the ember warm his side.

On earth Prometheus showed the glowing ember to several humans, who delighted in its powerful warmth. Soon they ignited logs and branches and sticks with the ember and passed the gift of fire from one to the other until the earth was lighted up by dancing flames.

It was now possible for men and women to cook their food and to gather around the fire to warm themselves. Prometheus instructed them on how to fashion tools from heated metal and how to make weapons.

Zeus soon spied one of the burning fires as he looked out on the world from his palace among the gods. Enraged, he summoned Prometheus before him.

"What have you done?" he screamed.

"I have given to humans the one thing they always should have owned," replied Prometheus.

"Then you shall be punished for your disobedience!" Zeus cried.

He ordered Prometheus to be taken to an outcrop of cliffs above the sea, and to be chained to the rocks. Every morning a giant eagle would descend from the clouds and attack the helpless Prometheus by devouring his liver. Every night Prometheus's liver would grow back in time to be consumed by the eagle after sunrise.

Prometheus endured this torture for centuries before he was eventually freed. Despite the ghastly punishment, Prometheus is fondly remembered for sharing the power of fire with humans on earth.

DESTRUCTION

Pandora's Box

The great god Zeus was the most powerful god in the Greek pantheon, or family, of gods that ruled the universe. Despite his wisdom and compassion for his creations, Zeus could be jealous, petty, and cruel. He punished his wife Hera for plotting to dethrone him, and was equally harsh with his sons and daughters.

When the god Prometheus angered Zeus by giving the gift of fire to humans on earth, Zeus had him chained to a cliff where an eagle would viciously attack him each day. But even this punishment did not satisfy Zeus, for he wished to inflict more pain on the humans, who now possessed the secret of fire.

Zeus thought of a very clever way to get revenge on the mortals and teach them a lesson. He asked his son, the god Hephaestus, who was an artisan to the gods, to sculpt a woman from clay. When Hephaestus had finished, Zeus took the sculpture to the goddess Athena and asked her to breathe life into it. Zeus called his creation "Pandora," or "all-endowed." From every god of Olympus, Pandora received many favorable gifts, such as the ability to sew, to entertain, and to cook. She was given beauty, grace, and charm. Her wardrobe was woven from precious metals and jewels, and flowers adorned her long blond hair.

Strange sounds and smells filled the air. Black-winged creatures poured forth from the box like a swarm of locusts.

Zeus was involved in a long-standing feud with the old gods or Titans of Greece. Part of his plot to teach the humans a lesson included taking revenge on the brother of Prometheus who was a Titan. Epimetheus was dim-witted and easily flattered, unlike his brother.

Zeus instructed Hermes, the messenger god, to deliver Pandora to Epimetheus. Before he sent her, however, he gave the beautiful woman a box, or a "dowry," which contained untold wealth.

"Do not open this box, Pandora," Zeus told her. "It is your dowry, which contains many, many treasures."

Pandora excitedly took the box from Zeus. She wondered what magnificent things it contained.

Hermes led Pandora to Epimetheus. When he first saw her, Epimetheus was overcome by Pandora's many charms. He could hardly take his eyes away from her. He lost all sense of logic. He forgot that he had been warned by his brother, Prometheus, not to accept gifts from Zeus. He even forgot that it was Zeus who held his poor brother in captivity, bound to the jagged cliffs above the sea. Epimetheus was too overtaken by the beauty and grace of Pandora.

Pandora was briefly occupied with all the attention she received from Epimetheus. She enjoyed the flattery and the compliments that he gave her, but the thrill of his advances did not remain with her for long. Soon she tired of it all. She began to think of the box that Zeus had given her. She wondered what it contained and why she was not allowed to open it. After all, it was her dowry. Didn't she have the right to show Epimetheus what was inside?

Innocently Pandora began to play with the lid of the box, gently prying it loose with her fingers. She wiggled the lock. Nothing happened. Finally, in frustration, she gave the lid a strong tug. It popped open.

Strange sounds and smells filled the air. Black-winged creatures poured forth from the box like a swarm of locusts. They filled the land and sky and spread across the water until the earth was darkened with their presence. The creatures were called "agony" and "pain," "suffering" and "regret." The earth had not known these things until Pandora opened the box that Zeus had given her. Now there was hunger and suffering everywhere. Children cried, and husbands and wives quarreled bitterly.

When Pandora realized what was happening, she tried to close the lid of the box. It was difficult to do, but after hours of struggling with it, she managed to slam it shut. Unfortunately, it seemed that all the ills of the world had escaped.

Epimetheus was horrified when he realized what Pandora had done. "Now no one will remember me as the brother of Prometheus who gave the world the gift of fire! They will only think of me as your husband—the husband of the woman who gave the world all its pain and misery!" Epimetheus was no longer charmed by Pandora. He left her alone.

However, Pandora looked closely at the box. One thing was not released from its contents. Just inside the lid a glimmer of hope remained imprisoned in the box. Pandora knew that it was important that she keep the lid sealed so that humans would never lose the gift of hope.

Looking down at her from his home with the gods, Hephaestus took pity on his lovely creation. He traveled to the earth and took Pandora back with him to Olympus.

Demeter and Persephone

Persephone was the beloved daughter of Demeter, the goddess of the harvest. She lived with her mother on the island of Sicily, off the coast of Italy. Every day Persephone would play among the vines of grapes and rows of grain that her mother had blessed. She was enchanted by the beauty of nature, the warmth of the sun, and the bounty of the earth. The people of Greece were grateful for Demeter's goodwill, for it assured a fruitful harvest.

One evening Persephone did not return to her mother after a day of playing in the fields. Demeter grew concerned. It was not like Persephone to come home late. Demeter began to search for her daughter. She asked everyone she met if they had seen Persephone, but no one could help her.

Finally Demeter appealed to Hekate, the goddess of the moon. "From your position high in the sky, Hekate, perhaps you've seen my Persephone."

Sadly, Hekate had not seen the girl. She suggested that Demeter go to the god Helios—ruler of the sun—and ask him. Demeter approached Helios, who was about to embark on his daily journey across the sky. Helios calmed the high-strung horses that were eager to pull his chariot, and listened to the pleas of Demeter.

"Your daughter has been abducted," he told Demeter. "Hades, god of the underworld, came upon Persephone while she was picking flowers. He has driven her in his carriage to the dark world beneath this world, where he wishes for her to sit next to him on his throne."

Demeter was heartbroken. She knew that the mighty god Zeus was aware of Hades's actions. This angered her so much that she refused to go to Olympus with the other gods at Zeus's request. She refused to bless the crops and promote a good harvest. All that concerned her was finding her daughter.

Demeter wandered aimlessly through town after town, lost in thought. She sat near a well one day and closed her eyes to rest. A local girl from the village saw Demeter by the well, but did not recognize the powerful goddess.

"Old woman," the girl asked, "why aren't you at home with your family at the end of this day? It's getting late."

Demeter did not answer.

"If you have nowhere to go," the girl continued, "please, come with me to my house. We have need of a nursemaid for my newborn brother."

Demeter was touched by the girl's concern. She followed her to her home and tended to the infant, who was called Demophon. In a short amount of time, Demeter's sorrows were softened by the baby's smiles. She grew attached to little Demophon and wished to bestow upon him the gods' gift of immortality.

As Demeter began the ceremony to give Demophon the right to eternal life, the baby's mother walked into the room. She saw Demeter lowering her child over an open flame and began to scream.

"No, no!" Demeter cried as the woman took Demophon away. "You shouldn't have done that! You misunderstand what I am trying to do."

With that, Demeter stood before Demophon's family and unveiled her fine robes and let her golden hair spill around her shoulders. Everyone gasped as they looked upon Demeter, for they realized that she was a goddess.

"I must leave you," Demeter told them. "I must continue my search for my own daughter, Persephone. But before I leave, I will bless your fields and they will continue to give you a bountiful harvest."

The ground sprang forth with all types of flowers and blossoms.
Young seedlings pushed through the dark soil to find the sunlight.

Demeter continued her sad journey alone. Everywhere she traveled, people begged her to bestow her powers of life on their crops. But Demeter refused.

The people finally appealed to Zeus for help. Afraid that Demeter's actions would stop the daily flow of offerings he received from the farmers, Zeus commanded Hades to release Persephone. He sent Hermes, the messenger god, to retrieve the girl. "As long as she has not eaten anything while in the realm of Hades, she may return to her mother," Zeus told Hermes.

Hermes traveled to the dark underworld and crossed the river Styx. He found Hades sitting on his throne, with a pale and undernourished Persephone by his side. Hermes told Hades what Zeus had commanded.

"Very well," Hades responded. "But you must know that Persephone has eaten the seeds of a pomegranate."

Demeter appealed to Zeus to intervene. She could not bear the idea that Persephone would remain forever with Hades in the underworld.

Zeus proclaimed that Persephone would stay with Hades as his bride for two-thirds of the year.

During the spring, however, she would be able to rejoin her mother.

This solution pleased Demeter, who celebrated her reunion with her daughter by placing her blessing on all growing things. The ground sprang forth with all types of flowers and blossoms. Young seedlings pushed through the dark soil to find the sunlight.

When Persephone returned to Hades, however, Demeter withdrew her magic from the earth. Then the trees dropped their leaves, and a snowy frost covered the ground, as Demeter waited again for her beloved daughter.

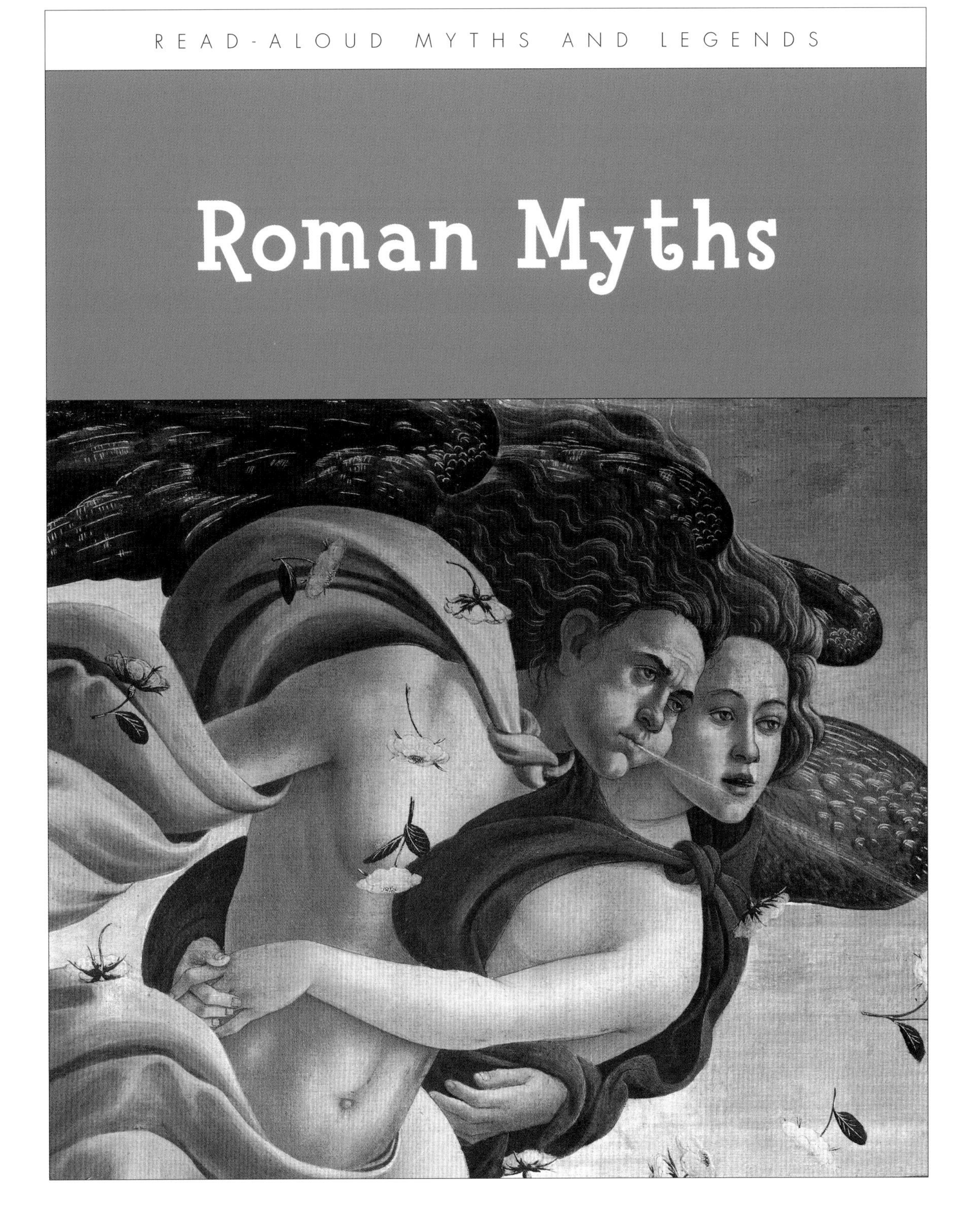
READ-ALOUD MYTHS AND LEGENDS
Roman Myths

The Golden Branch

When his ships touched shore in Italy, Aeneas went to locate the Sibyl. The ancient prophet was already hundreds of years old in the time of Aeneas. The god Apollo had given her the gift of prophecy and longevity. Though he gave her a very long life, Apollo deprived the Sibyl of everlasting youth and beauty because she refused to be his lover.

Aeneas hurried to the cave where he knew the Sibyl lived. The cave was set within a grove near a temple dedicated to Apollo and the goddess Diana. The warrior stood in reverence to the god and goddess for a few moments. He looked toward the opening of the cave and wondered whether the Sibyl would honor his request.

"Do not yield to the disasters, but press forward that much more bravely," said the ancient voice.

Aeneas had come to ask the Sibyl to accompany him to the Land of the Dead to visit his father, Anchises. He had been told in a dream to take the trip. According to the dream, his father would reveal Aeneas's future and the fortunes of the Roman people. Anchises would instruct Aeneas about how to fulfill his destiny.

The Sibyl began to speak of the Underworld before Aeneas even had the opportunity to state his request. In a trancelike state the prophet foretold of the difficulties and dangers on the road to his father. Many perils awaited Aeneas.

"I have prepared myself for these," said Aeneas.

"The descent is easy. The gate of Pluto is open night and day. The toil is to retrace your steps and return to the upper air," warned the Sibyl.

She told Aeneas he must procure a golden branch as a gift for Proserpine, queen of the Underworld. He would find it in the forest upon one of the trees. If his fate was to be prosperous, the tree would yield the branch easily. No force could tear the branch away. Even if it were possible to break the branch from the tree trunk by force, the effort would be wasted. If the branch was broken from the tree, someone other than the person who tore it off would succeed in that person's place.

Aeneas heeded the Sibyl's solemn words and set off for the forest. A short distance from the cave, he noticed two doves. They belonged to his mother, the goddess Venus. The doves directed Aeneas to the tree that bore the golden branch. The branch came easily away from the trunk when Aeneas touched it. He hurried back to the Sibyl with it.

In the region of volcanoes, near Mount Vesuvius, the countryside rippled with chasms. Flames of sulphur burst forth accompanied by hollow roars from the earth's foundation. In an extinct volcano lay Lake Avernus. The lake was half a mile wide and very deep. Beyond the volcano's steep banks was a dense, gloomy forest. No wildlife sweetened the area, and no birds flew overhead nor dared to light upon the strange trees.

The cave through which to enter the Underworld was on the lake's banks. At the direction of the Sibyl, Aeneas offered sacrifices to Proserpine, to Hecate (goddess of sorcery and Proserpine's attendant), and to the Furies, the spiteful female deities who existed to seek revenge. When he finished, the earth resounded with a great bellowing that shook the hilltops. Howling dogs announced the presence of the deities Aeneas had worshipped.

"Summon your courage. Now you will need it," proclaimed the Sibyl. She descended into the cave. Aeneas followed in her path.

They passed a cluster of beings, called Griefs, Cares, Diseases, Age, Fear, Hunger, Toil, Poverty, and Death. The beings were horrible to behold, and Aeneas had to look away. Next he saw monsters. Briareus had one hundred arms. The Hydras, with their huge dog-like bodies and many snake heads, hissed at him. The lion-headed, goat-bodied, serpent-tailed Chimeras breathed fire. Aeneas was so revolted that he drew his sword, but before he could strike, the Sibyl restrained him.

They moved on to the black river called Cocytus. The ferryman Charon was waiting. Charon was very old, but still strong. Eager to board the ferry were many and all types of passengers, including glorious heroes, young boys, and maidens with hair of all colors. The ferryman accepted only those passengers he chose.

The Sibyl explained the reason to Aeneas. "Charon takes only those passengers whose souls have received proper burial rites. The others must wander for a hundred years before he will take them."

When Charon saw Aeneas, he asked, "By what right do you approach this shore? You are armed and still alive."

"He will commit no violence," answered the Sibyl. "He wishes only to see his father, Anchises."

Aeneas held out the golden branch for Charon to observe. Seeing it, the ferryman turned his back to Aeneas and the Sibyl, and cooled his anger. After a few moments he invited them to board his boat. The ferry buckled under the weight of the living Aeneas, for it was so accustomed to transporting the light souls of the dead.

As the ferry approached the opposite shore, the three-headed dog Cerberus awaited them. His necks bristled with snakes. He held his ground, barking furiously out of all three throats. The Sibyl threw the dog a medicated cake, which he devoured. When Cerberus retired to his cave for a nap afterward, Aeneas and the Sibyl disembarked safely upon the far shore of the Underworld.

Cerberus

Aeneas in the Underworld

Aeneas and the ancient female prophet, the Sibyl, disembarked from the ferry on the shore of the Underworld. They sought Aeneas's father, Anchises. The first sound they heard were the wails of the children who had died at birth. Alongside the children were people who had been put to death under false charges. Minos, the son of Zeus and Europa, who had been king of Crete, acted as judge and heard each of the cases of the falsely accused.

Aeneas and the Sibyl next traveled past the souls of the people who had taken their own lives.

"How willingly would they now suffer poverty, hardship, and other inflictions if they could return to life," advised the Sibyl.

Aeneas felt the heaviness of sadness as they progressed. From the groves of myrtle trees, radiated numerous paths. On the paths humans who had been disappointed in love roamed endlessly. Even death had not cured their heartache. Could it be? Aeneas thought he saw the figure of Dido. She bore a recent wound. Dido had been queen of Carthage, and Aeneas's lover for one year before the god Mercury had instructed him to depart for Italy. At Aeneas's departure Dido killed herself with her own sword.

Aeneas felt the heaviness of sadness as they progressed.

"Could that be you, unhappy Dido? Was I the reason you perished? I left you only at the request of the gods. I did not think my absence would harm you so deeply. Please, do not refuse me one last farewell," cried Aeneas.

Dido continued to move on the path she had chosen. Momentarily she stopped and looked to the ground. Silently she began to walk again. Aeneas pursued her for a short distance. With a disappointed heart he turned around and rejoined the Sibyl.

They passed through the fields where the heroes who fell in battle gathered. The Trojan heroes flocked to the living Aeneas in his shiny armor. The Greeks, on the other hand, fled from him as they once had done on the plains of Troy. Aeneas wanted to linger with the dead Trojans, but the Sibyl hurried him away from the fields.

The road was divided at the next place they encountered. One road led to Elysium, the destination of the blessed. The other road progressed to the regions where the condemned dwelled. The fiery waters of the Phlegethon surrounded the walled city of the condemned. The avenging Fury Tisiphone kept watch from an iron tower by the gate. Tremendous groans emerged from the city. The creaking of iron and the clanking of chains rose from the background.

"What crimes have they committed?" Aeneas asked the Sibyl.

"This is the judgment hall of Rhadamantus, who illuminates the crimes that they thought they had hidden so well during their lifetime. Tisiphone whips them with scorpions. Then she hands the offenders over to her sister Furies," the Sibyl explained solemnly.

Just then, the gates flew open. Aeneas observed a Hydra with fifty heads guarding the entrance. Some of those inside sat at tables that were heavy with savory things to eat. A Fury stood ready to snatch away the food from the lips of anyone who dared to try to taste the delicacies. Over the heads of others were gigantic rocks that threatened to crush them at any moment. The Sibyl explained that these people had hated their siblings, injured their parents, or were disloyal to their friends when they were alive.

She pointed out several figures. One was Sisyphus. Time after time he rolled a tremendous stone up a hill until he almost reached the summit. Each time he was about to roll it up to the crest, a sudden force repelled the rock and pushed it back to the bottom of the hill.

She showed Tantalus to Aeneas. Thirsty, Tantalus stood in a pool of water up to his chin. Time after time he lowered his head to take a drink. When he did, the water disappeared beneath his feet. Around him were trees heavy with pears, pomegranates, apples, and plump figs. Whenever the hungry Tantalus reached to pluck a piece of the fruit, a fierce wind blew the fruit-laden branch out of his grasp.

"We must turn away from this region of the melancholy for the city of the blessed," advised the Sibyl.

Even as they traveled through the middle region of darkness, Aeneas was grateful. They emerged upon the Elysian Fields, where the souls of the happy rested. A purple light cloaked everything that Aeneas saw in these fields. The city of the blessed had its own sun and stars. Inhabitants played games on the grass. Others danced. Still others sang. The renowned musician and poet Orpheus played sweet music on his lyre for all to enjoy.

In a laurel grove, the source of the great River Po, Aeneas witnessed the founders of Troy. Nearby were their resplendent chariots and armor. Their horses freely roamed the plains. Here dwelled also the poets and priests who had sung the glories of the gods. Here, too, rested the people who had lived their lives in the service of humankind. Aeneas knew he would find his father, Anchises, nearby.

A Father's Message to His Son

The old woman prophet called the Sibyl led Aeneas to the city of the blessed in the Underworld. They traveled through the groves of the Elysian Fields and witnessed the souls and the trees there bathed in a purple hue. The place was called Elysium and it was the paradise where the souls that were saved went after death. The inhabitants were the founders of the Trojan state, old heroes, priests, and other blessed souls who contributed to the happiness of their fellow humans during their lives in the upper world. Strains of sweet music penetrated Elysium.

"Where is the soul called Anchises?" inquired the Sybil of a group of inhabitants.

The Sybil and Aeneas turned down to a rich, green valley. Under a tree sat Anchises. He was deep in thought until he recognized his son, Aeneas.

"You have come at last. I was contemplating posterity, my ancestors, and my descendants. I have worried over your well-being as you've lived the career of a hero of Troy," said Anchises to his son.

"My father! Your image guided me throughout my adventures," proclaimed Aeneas. He reached out to embrace his father. But his arms enfolded a mere image and not the substance of the body he remembered when Anchises was alive.

Aeneas soothed his disappointment by looking out over the wide, tranquil valley. A gentle summer wind danced through the trees. The River Lethe cut through the landscape like a ribbon. Aeneas noticed a multitude of forms on the far bank. They reminded him of the insects he might find on a summer's day on earth.

"Those souls will receive bodies in time. In the meantime they reside on the bank of the Lethe. They are engaged in drinking to obliviate their most recent lives. They must forget in order to be born fresh once more," explained Anchises.

"Father, how can it be possible for souls to love the upper world so much that they would depart from this tranquil valley?" asked Aeneas.

"I will relate for you the plan of creation in order to explain," answered his father.

Aeneas listened as Anchises told his story. "The Creator originally made souls from the four elements, which are fire, air, earth, and water. The four combined into the most excellent element, which is fire, and they became flame. The Creator scattered this flame like seed among the sun, moon, and stars.

"The inferior gods took the seed and made human beings and the other animals. To do this, they mixed in different proportions of earth to reduce the purity of the seed. The more earth they put into the composition of the human or animal, the less pure that individual became. You have seen that men and women in their adult bodies are far less pure than they were in their childhood.

"After death the impurity must be cleaned away. Souls purge away the earth that composed their bodies by airing themselves in the wind. Or by washing in water. Or by burning in the fire. Only a few souls like myself are immediately admitted to Elysium without cleansing. And only a few souls remain here forever.

"The rest of the souls return to earth again after they are cleansed of the impurities of their last life. They return with new bodies. And they return without any memory of the life before. That memory they have washed away in the River Lethe."

"What about the animals?" asked Aeneas.

"Some human souls have been so corrupted by their past deeds that they are unfit to return to the upper world in human bodies. These souls are reborn as the brute animals. They become lions, cats, monkeys and the like. The natives of India do not destroy the life of an animal, because the beast might be a relative in a different form," explained Anchises.

The father showed his son which of the souls waiting by the river would become his relatives in their next lives. Anchises related what these souls would accomplish on earth when they were born into new bodies. He shared with him what Aeneas himself would do when he returned to the upper world. He would fight battles and win wars. He would find a bride to wed and found the Trojan state. Out of that state, the Roman state would become the most powerful sovereign in the world.

It was time for Aeneas and the Sibyl to return to the upper world. They bid farewell to Anchises. The Sibyl led Aeneas back to earth through a secret shortcut.

"I will build a temple to your honor and bring you offerings," said Aeneas to the Sibyl upon their return.

"I am no goddess, nor do I have any claim to offerings," she answered. "I am a mortal. I did not accept the love of Apollo when he claimed me. Instead, I took a handful of sand and asked to see that many birthdays. Unfortunately, I forgot to ask for eternal youth. So far, I have lived seven hundred years. I have still to experience three hundred springs and three hundred harvests. In time I will be lost to sight. But my voice will stay behind, and future peoples will respect my words."

Juno Versus the Destiny of Aeneas

Juno was the goddess of women and marriage. She was married to Jupiter, ruler of the worlds of gods and humans. The Trojan hero Aeneas was part mortal and part immortal, having the human father Anchises and the goddess of love, Venus, as his mother. He was to become the father of the Roman people. But Juno tried to stop him for a number of reasons.

It all began at the wedding of Peleus and Thetis. Thetis was one of the fifty Nereids, or sea nymphs, and a daughter of the minor sea god Nereus and the sea goddess Doris. Jupiter himself had once wooed Thetis. But when the god learned that her future son was to become greater than his father, he decided that Thetis should marry a mortal. Jupiter chose Peleus, king of Phthia, to wed Thetis.

Nearly all the gods and goddesses attended the wedding. But Eris, the goddess of discord, however, was not invited. To cause havoc Eris inscribed "For the Fairest Goddess" upon a Golden Apple. She threw the Golden Apple into the reception. Immediately a dispute arose among Juno, Venus, and Minerva, the latter being the goddess of wisdom and war.

"Surely, this is meant for me," proclaimed Juno.

"Absolutely not. It is mine," declared Venus.

"I own this Golden Apple," boasted Minerva.

Jupiter ordered the goddesses to take their dispute to the walled city of Troy, which was located on the coast of the Aegean Sea in Asia Minor. He selected Paris, the very handsome Trojan prince, to decide which goddess deserved the Golden Apple. One by one the three goddesses tried to bribe the prince.

"Choose me and you'll rule the world," declared Juno.

"You'll be victorious in every battle if you name me," offered Minerva.

"Select me and you'll have the most beautiful woman in the world," tempted Venus. She referred to the notoriously beautiful Helen, who was also a daughter of Jupiter.

Juno

Paris awarded the Golden Apple to Venus without hesitation. Unfortunately, Helen was married to the Greek king of Sparta. His name was Menelaus. Paris stealthily made off to Troy with Queen Helen while he was a guest in the house of Menelaus. Juno now had two reasons to hate Aeneas. He was the son of her rival Venus and he was from the same land as Paris.

King Menelaus named his brother Agamemnon as commander-in-chief of the forces he organized to wage war against Troy. The bloody war would end with the surprise defeat of Troy by the Greeks, who hid inside the wooden Trojan Horse and tricked the Trojans into admitting them inside their city.

Aeneas served under Prince Hector, the leader of the Trojan forces, during the war. He escaped from the siege of Troy with his lame father upon his shoulders. He held his son Iulus and his wife Creusa by the hands. During their escape his wife was lost and was never found. Aeneas now led the only Trojan survivors in a fleet of twenty ships to search for a new home. It would take him nearly ten years to find a home in the land that is now Italy.

As Aeneas neared the end of his journey to his destined land, Juno took her revenge. She had added one more gripe against him. The city of Carthage was her favorite city. It was located south of Rome, across the Mediterranean Sea on the northern shore of Africa. Juno looked into the future and saw that the Roman descendants of Aeneas would destroy Carthage.

Aeolus obediently commissioned his sons, Boreas and Typhon, and the other winds, to fiercely toss the ocean in all directions.

Only Neptune retaliated against Juno's orders.

"In heavenly minds, resentments such as mine dwell deeply," vowed Juno to herself.

The goddess commanded Aeolus, the keeper of the winds, to destroy the Trojan fleet. Aeolus obediently commissioned his sons, Boreas and Typhon, and the other winds, to fiercely toss the ocean in all directions. The Trojan ships were set wildly off course. It looked like they would be destroyed.

Only Neptune retaliated against Juno's orders. He had not sanctioned the disturbance, and he was annoyed by the goddess's interference in his realm. Raising his head above the waves, he was able to see the Trojan fleet. He reprimanded the winds. He soothed the waves. And he swept away the clouds that obscured the face of the sun. He took up his trident, the three-pronged spear of the god of the sea, and he pried the ships off the rocks upon which they had been thrown. Neptune's son Triton, a minor sea god, and one of the sea nymphs lifted the other endangered ships upon their shoulders and steered them to safety. In this miraculous way, all of the Trojan ships were saved.

Aeneas was to wander for several more years. At long last his Trojan ships touched upon the shore of the land called Latium. King Latinus had a daughter named Lavinia. He had been told by an oracle that she would marry a foreign prince, so Latinus welcomed Aeneas and his countrymen.

The path was clear for Aeneas to marry the princess, except that Juno was not through with her revenge. One of the spiteful Furies, who was called Alecto, brewed up trouble between the Latins and the Trojans at the goddess's command. Alecto spoke against Aeneas to Lavinia's mother and nephew Turnus. Turnus was the king of the neighboring state of Ardea. He had wooed Lavinia for some years, so he declared war against Latium. When a single-handed battle was fought between Turnus and Aeneas, finally Juno did nothing to interfere. With a single blow Aeneas killed Turnus, and the war ended.

Aeneas married Lavinia and became the new king of Latium. Iulus, his Trojan son, succeeded his father to the throne. Other sons of Aeneas also ruled, including Silvius, the first child of the new Roman race. The line of Iulus was called the Julian House. Among the rulers to follow in this house for the next four centuries were Julius Caesar and Augustus Caesar.

Jupiter honored the request of Venus to have her son Aeneas become immortal. Once his mortality was cleansed in the waters of the sea, Aeneas became the minor god called Indiges.

You can see that this myth contains some history of Rome and its rulers. The poet Virgil created his hero Aeneas within the world of the gods and their powers in order to emphasize the importance of the Roman state.

The Children of Mars

Alba Longa was an ancient Latin city, which named itself in honor of the dawn. It was situated along a ridge behind which the sun seemed to rise each day. Silvius was the first king to reign in Alba Longa. His name came from the Latin word for forest, which is where he was born. Silvius was the son of Aeneas and Lavinia, and he was the first child of the new people who were to be known as Romans.

After Silvius died, two kings also took his forest name. These were Aeneas Silvius and Latinus Silvius. Proca was the next king, and his reign was supposed to pass to his son Numitor. But the succession of the throne from one king to the next within the Silvan dynasty stopped moving smoothly after Proca's death.

Numitor had an evil brother called Amulius. When Proca died, Amulius drove his brother, Numitor, the rightful heir to the throne, from the royal house. He then ordered Numitor's young sons to be killed. The maiden Rhea Silvia was the last of his brother's children. As evil as he was, Amulius was afraid to have Rhea Silvia killed. He knew the people of Alba Longa would turn against him if he ordered the death of an innocent maiden.

Amulius disposed of Rhea Silvia in a different way, seeing to it that she never married nor had any children. To make certain that no heir of Numitor's would someday challenge his right to rule, Amulius placed his niece among the women who did not marry. Rhea Silvia became a Vestal Virgin, one of the women who tended the sacred fire of Vesta, the goddess of hearth and home. Amulius told everyone that he did this as a means of honoring his brother's daughter, and the people believed him.

One day, while she went about her duties as a Vestal Virgin in the woods, Rhea Silvia came upon a man. A wolf and a woodpecker accompanied him. The man was Mars, the war god, and he forced Rhea Silvia to marry him. Because she broke her vow never to marry, Rhea Silvia was condemned to death by her uncle, who gladly took the opportunity to be rid of the last of his brother's children. Amulius had one more decree. While in prison, Rhea Silvia had given birth to twin boys. The angry king ordered the babies to be drowned in the river.

In the old days the river was called the Albula. After King Tiberinus of Alba was drowned there, its name was changed to the Tiber. In the time of the year when Rhea Silvia gave birth, the Tiber spread beyond its banks, creating shallow, stagnant pools. When the slaves of Amulius brought the twin boys to the river, they left the basket that held the babies among the grasses on the banks. When the water resumed its normal flow, the basket rested in the mud that remained.

A she-wolf found the babies inside, and she gave them some of her milk to drink. A woodpecker dropped food into their small mouths. The wolf and the woodpecker had saved the babies at the request of the infants' father, Mars.

Sometime later, a shepherd named Faustulus came upon the basket. He brought the twins to his hut, where they grew as his own children. The youngsters, who were named Romulus and Remus, were not content to be only with their sheep. As the sons of Mars, they ventured, too, over the mountains and through the forest during their days. Other boys accompanied them, and the twins became the leaders among their peers. They hunted wild beasts. They attacked gangs of robbers, took the spoil, and shared it.

Romulus, Remus, and the other boys attended the festival of the Lupercalia, on the hill now called Palatine. A gang of robbers, avenging the booty taken from them, stole Remus. Romulus followed from a distance, and he saw Remus thrown into the king's prison.

"My brother is in the prison of King Amulius," Romulus told the shepherd Faustulus.

"I have something to tell you, my son," answered Faustulus. "I was once the shepherd of Numitor. I saw him driven from his throne by his wicked brother. I witnessed the murder of his sons and the death of his daughter. Since you and your brother were babies, I have wondered when I would tell you. I see now is the time."

And Faustulus explained to Romulus that he had found a basket with two babies. He believed that the boys were of royal blood. But he had sheltered them because of the wrath of Amulius. He told Romulus that he and his brother were, in all likelihood, the grandsons of Numitor. And he sent him to speak with Numitor.

One look at his grandson told Numitor, who was now an old man, that Romulus belonged to the line of Silvan kings. Numitor swore to help him free his brother. They devised a plan.

Romulus and his shepherd friends armed themselves and went to Amulius's house. Numitor had traveled ahead of them. He told the king's defenders that enemies were invading the citadel, the fortress that protected the city. When the king's guards rushed to the citadel to prevent the feigned invasion, the shepherd boys freed Remus from prison. Amulius had no army to protect him, and Romulus slew him for his evil deeds against the family of Numitor.

The people hailed Numitor as their rightful king. They recognized Romulus and Remus to be of the royal house. For their part, Romulus and Remus swore allegiance to their grandfather and vowed to serve him.

The Founding of Rome

Romulus and Remus lived with their grandfather, King Numitor, in Alba Longa. But they were young, and Alba Longa was crowded. The brothers decided to found a new city. They shared their plan with the young men whom they had known when they lived with the shepherd Faustulus and his wife in the days before they were reunited with their grandfather.

The group of shepherd youth, with Romulus and Remus as their leaders, chose for their city the hills where they were accustomed to grazing their sheep and the open spaces surrounded by woods where they chased robbers and hunted game. Romulus selected Palatine Hill for his quarters. Remus took Aventine Hill for his.

Remus received the first augury, a sign that was believed at the time to predict the future. One day he saw a flight of six vultures. The vulture was considered a sacred bird because it did not prey on other birds, but only fed on dead things.

"Surely, I am the one destined to found the city and give it a name," exclaimed Remus to Romulus and the shepherds.

Nearly as soon as Remus had spoken the words, Romulus observed a flight of twelve vultures!

"It is I who has been selected. I saw twice the number," boasted Romulus.

Immediately he set out to build a wall around the city to protect it, convinced that it was indeed he whom the gods had chosen. Remus ridiculed his brother. Laughing, he leaped over the wall into the city. Romulus struck down Remus and killed him on the spot.

"So will perish all who leap over my walls," declared the proud Romulus.

He called the city Rome after himself and became its king. But the city of Rome had very few people. The surrounding population had shown no interest in joining the followers of Romulus and Remus in the new city.

So Romulus founded a sanctuary between two groves partly up the slope that is now called Capitoline Hill. He invited men who had committed dangerous crimes to the sanctuary. He also sent the word out that debtors who could not meet their obligations were welcome. Anyone who was being pursued for whatever reason could come. What the newcomers would find in the sanctuary, promised Romulus, was safety and protection.

The population of the new city upon the hills soon became a strong and daring bunch. Now there was another problem. Few women resided in the city of Rome. The fugitives did not have wives, and without the birth of children the city would not endure.

Ancient Rome

Romulus sent messengers throughout the land to the neighboring states and cities. He asked the heads of the states and cities to enter into marriage alliances with the men of his city. But the neighboring rulers and peoples considered Rome to be more a camp of outcasts than a city that deserved their respect. In fact, it could be said that most of them wished the city to perish for its lawlessness.

One neighbor responded, "Unless you have a sanctuary for runaway women, you'll have no wives."

The statement drew the wrath of Romulus and the residents of Rome. Romulus became determined to find wives for the men through trickery and force. It was the time for the harvest and the festival of Consus, the god who helped the people to gather and store their crops. Romulus sent an official invitation to the people of the closest neighboring state. He promised a great spectacle if they attended the celebration of the festival of Consus in Rome.

The neighbors Romulus invited were the Sabines. Despite their dislike of the Romans, they could not resist a good spectacle. The Sabines came to Rome in droves. Most of the men brought their wives and children. When they arrived, they marveled at the wall around the new city and at the new building that had been constructed. The Romans invited the Sabines to stay with them in their houses, and they treated their guests to all manner of food, drink, games, and music. The Sabines began to lose their distrust of the residents of the new city.

The day of the spectacle dawned at last. Finely clad, young Roman men seated upon wondrous horses delighted the crowd. They paraded the horses in formation and demonstrated how well the animals responded to command. The crowd applauded and cheered for more. But the spectacle changed from the parade to something unexpected.

On cue the horsemen galloped among the Sabines. The surprised crowd scattered in all directions. Parents and older brothers did not have time to protect the young women. One by one, the Sabine maidens were swooped up by the young Romans on horseback, who desired them as wives.

"A curse on this city for the crime of violating the code of hospitality," said the spokesman for the Sabines.

Romulus dispatched a messenger to the Sabine king. He promised that the maidens would be given an honorable ceremony of marriage. They would then share in the riches of Rome. As for the Roman husbands, Romulus himself would see that they consoled their wives for the loss of their home and families. What Romulus promised did come to be. The maidens were treated respectfully by their new husbands after a proper ceremony. But, back in their land, the Sabine fathers donned the robes of mourning and stirred up the sympathy of the people, who vowed to punish the Roman people for the crime.

The Sibyl

An old woman presented herself at the court of King Tarquin the Proud. Wrinkles that could only have been earned over many centuries traced her face. A wooden staff supported her. Heavy gray hair lay like a tremendous weight upon her shoulders. Under one arm she held a large, cumbersome bundle. Her eyes glowed with light and purpose.

"Bring me before the king," said the old woman at the door of the king's house.

"You have no place here," responded the doorkeeper.

"I must see the king," demanded the woman.

King Tarquin the Proud was seated upon his throne when the doorkeeper startled him with news of the insistence of the would-be visitor. The doorkeeper described the woman's aged countenance. The king had dreamed the evening before of an ancient woman, whom he did not know, but who matched in appearance the woman of whom the doorkeeper spoke. Neither the king nor the servant knew that she was a prophet. The god Apollo himself had given her the power of prophecy. He had also bestowed upon her the gift of a very long life. Apollo had offered her youth and beauty, too, if she would have agreed to become his mistress. But the woman, who was called the Sibyl, had refused Apollo's request.

The king, robed in purple and seated upon his ivory chair, with his protectors about him, pondered the situation a moment. Then he instructed the servant to admit the stranger. She proceeded, supported by her staff and carrying her great bundle, until she stood directly before Tarquin the Proud. She opened the bundle and carefully extracted its contents. She held before the king nine books.

"These books I would sell to you, O King," she said.

Her voice quaked when she spoke. The sound alarmed all those who were present. They could not discern whether the strangeness was because she had not used the voice in a very long time. Or, was it due to the fact that this woman was not like any human they had ever encountered.

"What do your books contain?" asked Tarquin the Proud.

"A foretelling of the events that will occur and how to deal with the events for the safety and greatness of Rome," answered the Sibyl in her shaky, hollow voice.

"What is the cost of your nine books?" the king demanded.

"Half of the king's treasury," she responded.

"Preposterous! You crazy old crone," ridiculed the king.

The woman asked that the brazier of burning coals in the room be brought to her. The king nodded to several people in the room to carry it over. Then she lifted three books from the pile. With surprising strength she threw the books into the fire. Everyone in the room watched as the flames consumed the volumes. They observed the burning until the leaves turned to ashes.

Once more the woman, who was now leaning more heavily upon her staff than she had before, spoke in the strange voice. "I have books for sale. It is for you to buy them, O King."

"How much, then, do you ask for the six remaining books?" demanded King Tarquin the Proud.

"Half of the king's treasury," she responded.

"That is what you asked when you had nine books," said Tarquin.

"I ask the same price for six as I did for nine," insisted the woman.

"She must be the craziest woman in Rome," said one of the king's advisors.

"She is not from Rome," corrected another advisor.

"Indeed, she is a stranger," said someone else.

"I cannot pay the price you ask for your books or anyone's books," roared the king.

The Sibyl took three books from her pile of six, lifting them above her head for all in the room to see. The flames lit up her aged face so that every wrinkle captivated their eyes. Assured that she held everyone's attention, she cast the three books into the brazier. Tarquin looked at her with respect.

"Half of your treasury, O King, for the three books that are not yet burned," said the Sibyl.

Laughter filled the room, but the king did not join the others in the merriment. He knew that once she threw the last three books into the flames, he would never see this woman again. The realization filled him with worry. He told her to come closer. She hobbled toward him until she stood next to his ivory chair.

"Leave the books. For your payment you will take half of the king's treasury," commanded Tarquin the Proud.

The keepers of the treasury escorted the Sibyl to the treasury. When she had departed with her payment, the king ordered the last three volumes to be put into a shrine in the temple of Jupiter. Fifteen priests guarded them for one thousand years. The priests' duty was to consult the books whenever the Romans had the need to speak with the gods regarding the welfare of their city. The books were called the Sibyline Books, after the woman who brought them to Rome.

Psyche and Cupid

Psyche was the youngest of three daughters born to the king and queen of a faraway country. Her beauty was so great that any of the words that were spoken to describe her appearance sounded empty and meaningless. Men came from great distances, not as suitors but as worshippers, to gaze upon her. Rumor spread that Venus had left her immortal home in heaven to become mortal in the form of the girl named Psyche. Shrines to Venus soon emptied of the mortal worshippers now enthralled with Psyche. Before long, Venus got word of the happenings.

"Shall I who am judged the fairest among the immortal goddesses be challenged by an earthly girl? This Psyche will have little joy from her loveliness," she challenged.

Venus called her son Cupid to her. He was the winged boy who flew at night, armed with his bows and arrows, inflicting the pain of love upon unsuspecting mortals. Venus and Cupid traveled together to the faraway country to observe Psyche.

"I pray you, allow your mother a fitting vengeance. See to it that this Psyche becomes slave to an unworthy love," Venus instructed Cupid.

Once his mother was off to her purposes, Cupid wounded himself with his own arrow, so overcome was he with the maiden's loveliness. For her part, Psyche was desperate with the attentions of so many men. Her sisters had both wedded before they reached Psyche's age. Psyche fell into a deep sorrow.

Psyche

Her parents left at once to consult an oracle about their youngest daughter's future. "Dress the maiden for a wedding and for death. Place her on top of a mountain. Do not search for a son-in-law of mortal blood. Her husband will be the serpent whom even the gods fear, who makes the bodiless ones on the Styx shrink in terror," said the oracle.

Beneath her yellow veil Psyche wept. The torch that was lighted upon the mountain gathered ashes, and an ominous dark smoke replaced it. What should have been the joyous strain of the pipe sounded like a wail. Psyche's family held their heads low as they would at a funeral.

"Do not waste your tears by weeping for me," Psyche told them. And she said goodbye and asked them to leave her alone upon the mountaintop.

When they had departed, the gentle breeze Zephyrus lifted Psyche from her perch. He set her softly among the flowers in the valley beneath the mountain. When Psyche awoke, she saw a fountain as clear as ice next to a golden dwelling place supported by golden pillars and ivory arches. Silver latticed the walls. The wild creatures of the wood frolicked about the dwelling, and the air hung with the music of more birds than Psyche had ever heard.

Psyche entered the house, sure that it was the abode of a god who had rescued her from a miserable life. A banquet was laid in the great room. Beautiful goblets and vessels adorned the table. A multitude of fine tastes and textures presented themselves for her pleasure.

A voice said, "Lady and mistress! I am your servant. This is your feast, which is fit for a queen." No one appeared to claim the voice or to share the feast.

She heard a song played by harp and sung to honor her, but the bearer of the song was invisible. Unseen hands lit the lamps. When she finished eating, the same unseen hands extinguished the light. Exhausted, Psyche wandered to her bed. Her bridegroom came to her, but he departed before the dawn.

During the next day and the days that followed, Psyche was cared for as she had been the day of her arrival. One evening her husband spoke to her for the first time. "Psyche, my life and my spouse! Ill-favored fortune at the hands of mortals is harkening toward us. Your sisters are seeking after you. You will hear their cries. If you must, answer them. But do not yield to their counsel about my form. If you do, we may never embrace each other again."

The gentle breeze Zephyrus lifted Psyche from her perch.

Psyche wept at his words. To live without him would break her heart. Trustingly, she admitted her sisters to her dwelling. They marveled at the luxuries that belonged to her. And they were very jealous. While they had been properly married by arrangement as was the custom of the time, their husbands were poor by comparison. They prodded Psyche about the location of her husband. She responded that he was away hunting. But they knew she was withholding something from them.

"Let us scare her, if not into revealing the secrets that live here, then at least we can bring her down from her high spirits," said the oldest sister. The other sister agreed with the plan.

"You exist in the midst of a danger you know nothing about. You have never seen your husband. We know that. Remember what the oracle spoke. You are destined to be devoured by none other than a beast. The beast waits for you to bear a babe so he can devour both of you. While nothing can be done to save you, at least know that we have warned you," said the sisters. They took turns saying the words.

That night Psyche bore their false message in her heart. While she was alone, she hid a knife in her bed for protection. Behind her curtain she concealed a lighted lamp. When her husband was sleeping soundly, Psyche arose from the bed. She held the knife in her right hand above her head, ready to strike him if necessary. She suspended the lighted lamp over the form of her husband.

Before her, she saw Love himself. She trembled at the sight of his golden hair, his soft, ruddy cheeks, and his white throat. His skin was fresh with dew. At his feet lay his bow and arrow. Psyche bent to kiss his red lips. A drop of the burning oil from the lamp fell upon his shoulder and burned him. Understanding at once his wife's faithlessness, Cupid rose from the bed and flew away.

Psyche and Venus

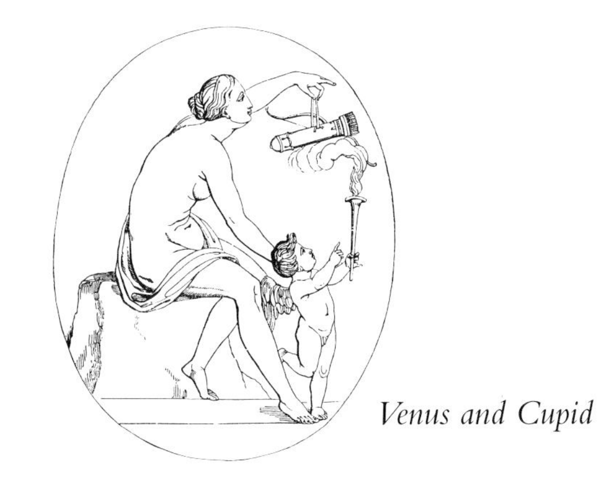

Venus and Cupid

The goddess of love, Venus, cursed the mortal maiden called Psyche because the girl's beauty was claiming the attention of the godddess's mortal worshippers. Hoards of foolish men flocked to the home of Psyche to gaze upon her, instead of paying their respects at the shrines of the goddess. So the angry Venus demanded that Psyche become the slave to an unworthy love. She entrusted her son Cupid, the boy god of love, to carry out her mission. But Cupid fell in love with Psyche. He enticed her to a beautiful palace filled with luxurious things. In the evenings he treated her like his queen. The only condition Cupid placed upon the arrangement was that Psyche promise never to investigate what he looked like. When Psyche, encouraged by her jealous sisters, broke this vow, the god of love fled from her.

This is a myth about how Psyche confronted the anger of Venus. No immortal being would give her aid outright because Venus was one of the most venerated immortals. However, Psyche did receive help from the blessed forces of nature in fulfilling the impossible tasks that Venus put before her.

Poor Psyche wandered from the castle in search of her husband, her heart aching for him. One day she came upon a temple. She looked inside for Cupid. What she saw instead were ears of wheat and barley strewn on the temple's floor, as well as sickles and other tools.

"While I am overcome with my desire for my husband, I must not neglect the shrine of any god or goddess," she said to herself.

So Psyche tidied up the shrine, putting everything in order. The goddess of the harvest, Ceres, came upon Psyche at the shrine. She knew the visitor as the wife of Cupid.

"While Venus tracks you, noble Psyche, I find you here in my service," said Ceres.

"Please, Goddess, conceal me here until I can recover some strength after my long wandering," pleaded Psyche.

But so adamant was the wrath of Venus, that Ceres refused. Psyche had no recourse but to continue on the journey to find her husband. She came upon a second shrine. This one was richly adorned with offerings and priceless garments. In the trees letters of gold spelled the name Juno, the great goddess of women and marriage. Psyche entered the temple and lay herself upon its altar in prayer.

"O Juno, spouse of Jupiter, you who are the helper in childbirth. Deliver me, Goddess, from the danger I face," prayed Psyche.

Juno answered, "If only I could answer your prayer, but I cannot. Venus is one I have loved as a daughter. I will not go against her wishes."

Leaving the temple of Juno, Psyche decided to face Venus directly. When she arrived at Venus's house, the servants mocked her. One of them dragged her by the hair to their mistress.

"You dare at last to greet me as your mother-in-law!" laughed Venus. "I will see whether you are a dutiful daughter-in-law."

The goddess took heaps of barley, millet, and every other grain she had in her fields and mixed them together into a tremendous mound. Then she sent Psyche to sort out one grain from the next into neat piles. Psyche knew the task was impossible and could do nothing but stare at the giant mound. After some moments an ant who had watched her all morning spoke.

"I have harnessed an army of ants to help you, wife of Love," said the ant.

When Venus returned that evening to find the grain carefully sorted, she was certain that her son had helped Psyche. She ordered the mortal as her next task to gather shreds of gold from the fleece of sheep that grazed on the land found on the other side of a rushing river.

Early the following morning Psyche came upon the torrent. It was useless to try to win the forgiveness of Venus, she thought. She was about to cast herself into the river to drown, when she heard a whisper.

"Dear Psyche, stop before you poison this water with self-destruction. Instead, rest beneath the plane tree until nightfall. You will find shreds of fleece left in the trees by the flock," said the whisper. It belonged to the green reed, the maker of music.

When Psyche gathered the shreds according to the reed's instruction and presented them to Venus, the goddess once again suspected that Cupid had given his assistance. She handed Psyche a crystal vessel. With her other hand she pointed to a high mountain.

"I am not finished with you yet. A dark stream runs down from the peak of that tall mountain. You must fill this crystal with water from its innermost source," demanded Venus.

Psyche climbed the mountain, fighting to keep her footing on its treacherous slope. At the top she found a rocky gulf that was invisible from the mountain's foot. Serpents with long necks and eyes that never blinked jutted out from among the rocks.

They spoke to Psyche in voices muffled by their surroundings. "Why did you come here?" hissed one of them.

"You are bringing destruction upon yourself," echoed the chorus of serpents.

Psyche lost any sense of purpose. Fatigue and despair filled her veins. She stood at the edge of the gulf as though she were of the same substance as the rock.

The eagle that belonged to Jupiter, the ruler of all gods, took pity on her. He swooped down for the crystal vessel and flew with it to the source of the stream. Filling it, he returned to Psyche.

"Go to Venus," said the eagle.

The serpents raised their heads and hissed, but they were unable to stop Psyche. Her legs were hers again. She raced down the strange mountain and gave the spiteful Venus the water she demanded.

Psyche in Hades

The goddess of love, Venus, was angry with the beautiful mortal named Psyche. Cupid, the son of Venus, and the boy god of love, had pierced himself with his own arrow in order to fall in love with her. Now Venus had a daughter-in-law against her wishes. She resolved to put Psyche to a test that would most likely kill her. Venus sent her to the Kingdom of the Dead, named for, and ruled by, the god Hades.

"Take this tiny casket to Proserpine, the queen of Hades. Tell her that Venus wishes for her to fill it with enough of her beauty to use for one day. Bring the casket back to me when she has filled it," Venus ordered Psyche.

Psyche understood that Venus intended to send her to her death. She set out for the tower she could see in the distance. Climbing to the top, she prepared to jump. Thus, she would quickly enter the Kingdom of the Dead.

"Wretched Psyche! If you die in the jump, which you surely will, you will indeed enter Hades. But you will never be able to return," scolded the stones of the tower.

"What does it matter whether I enter alive or dead. I will never accomplish what Venus demands," complained Psyche.

"I will guide you in what you must do," said the tower. "But you must not go empty-handed. Find two morsels of barley bread, one for each hand. Soak the bread in honey. Procure two pieces of money. Hold both in your mouth." Psyche listened carefully and obtained what the tower described. She departed for Hades further armed with the tower's instructions.

Not far into her journey, as the tower had said, Psyche came upon a mountain. She searched until she found an opening in the mountain's side. Through the hole she traveled the rough, dark course downward until she emerged in Hades. She looked for the castle of Orcus in the distance, like the tower had instructed. She walked in its direction. On the path she came face-to-face with a lame donkey carrying wood. The animal was driven by a lame master.

"Kind mortal, please hand me the cords that have slipped from the donkey's pack. If you do not, the burden he carries will be lost," implored the lame man.

But Psyche ignored him as the stones of the tower had directed her. She passed the man and the donkey in silence, then continued toward the River of the Dead, called the Styx. The ferryman Charon, who transported the dead across the river, ferried Psyche to the other side. As they came close to the far shore, an old man rose partially from the water and begged Psyche to help him into the boat. She was careful not to pity him, as the tower had instructed. When the ferry beached on the far shore, Psyche edged one of the two pieces of money out between her lips, and the ferryman grasped it with his fingers in payment.

"Lend us a hand in our spinning," cried a group of women with long, gray hair.

Psyche knew from the tower that if she helped them, she would have to drop one of the two pieces of bread she carried. She ignored their pleas and held fast to the bread that she would need to survive Hades. Psyche drew near at last to the isolated house of Proserpine. A watchdog bared his teeth at the entrance. Psyche gave one piece of the honey-soaked bread to the dog, and he closed his fierce mouth long enough for her to enter the house.

"What is it that has brought you to Hades?" asked Proserpine, the queen.

"I have come from Venus to ask you to fill this casket with beauty to last a day," answered Psyche.

"Have a seat while I do as Venus has requested," invited Proserpine.

When the queen took leave to stock the casket in private, Psyche sat upon the floor. She did not sit upon the couch, nor did she eat or drink anything that was left for her. To have done either would have confined her forever to the Kingdom of the Dead. When Proserpine returned, she handed Psyche the casket with the lid shut fast. At the door of the house, Psyche gave the watchdog the other piece of barley bread soaked in honey. She paid the ferryman Charon with the remaining piece of money when he left her on the opposite shore.

Psyche emerged from the vent of the mountain into the light of life. She rushed to the house of Venus with the casket filled with the beauty of Proserpine. An impulse to raise the lid and touch herself with a speck of dust from the beauty it held, and thus please Cupid, rose in Psyche. But when she opened the casket, its content was only sleep. And it was the sleep of the dead that felled Psyche to the ground. She could not move.

At that moment Cupid flew from the house of Venus, where he had been healing himself. With the point of one of his arrows, the god of love woke his mortal wife from the deep sleep. He ascended to the highest heavens and presented himself to Jupiter, ruler of the gods.

"You have upset the harmony of things," scolded Jupiter. Then he kissed Cupid's face. Jupiter commissioned his messenger Mercury to call the gods and goddesses together for a wedding. Once the immortals were assembled, Jupiter sent Mercury for Psyche.

"Drink this and live forever, married, with Cupid," said Jupiter to Psyche.

READ-ALOUD MYTHS AND LEGENDS
Celtic Myths

Nuada of the Silver Hand

IRELAND

The people of Dana were called Tuatha De Dannan, which means "the folk of the god whose mother is Dana." The goddess Dana had another name, Brigit. To the race that was mothered by Dana belonged the powers of Light and Knowledge. Later, in the history of Ireland, in the sixth century, the Christian St. Brigit was said to possess many of the qualities of the goddess Dana, or Brigit.

Dana was daughter of the god Dagda, or The Good. She had three sons. According to the ancient myths, the three sons had one son in common called Ecne, for "Knowledge" or "Poetry." Ecne, then, was said to be the son of Dana, because he came from her lineage.

The Dannans came to earth in a magic cloud. The cloud landed them in the land of Ireland in the location of Western Connacht. When the cloud cleared, the tribe called the Firbolgs discovered the Dannans in one of their fortresses. So they dispatched a warrior named Streng to investigate the new people who were in their fortress.

The Dannans sent the warrior Bres to meet Streng. When they stood face-to-face, the two warriors inspected each other's weapons.

"Yours are light and sharp-pointed," said the Firbolg Streng.

"Yours are so heavy and blunt," answered the Dannan Bres.

Bres then suggested, "Shall we not divide the land of Ireland equally between our peoples? We can then join together to defend it against future newcomers."

Streng told Bres he would have to bring the offer to the Firbolgs before he could answer. When he told his people about the Dannan's weaponry and what Bres had suggested, the Firbolgs were not moved by the Dannan's superiority. They refused the offer, and they decided to wage a battle for control of the land.

The two peoples met on the Plain of Moytura, or The Plain of the Towers, in the south of County Mayo, in what is now called Cong. King mac Erc led the Firbolgs. Nuada of the Silver Hand, who got his name from this very battle, led the Dannans. The Dannans used their magical powers and won the battle. During the fight the Firbolg king was slain. When Nuada's hand was severed, one of the Dannan metal crafters made the warrior a new hand of silver.

An agreement followed the battle. The Firbolgs were given the province of Connacht to rule. The rest of Ireland went to the Dannans. As the leader of the Dannan forces, Nuada of the Silver Hand was the rightful king of Ireland. But the Dannans chose Bres, since their laws forbid anyone with a blemish from ruling. King Bres was a different Bres from the warrior who had met with Streng before the battle.

King Bres was indeed strong, and he showed great physical beauty. Yet, King Bres had no talent for ruling. His mistakes caused new battles with the Fomorians, the ancient enemies of Ireland. He also taxed his subjects heavily and offered no hospitality to the chiefs, nobles, and harp players of the land. The Dannans considered lack of hospitality and generosity to be the worst vices a ruler could possess.

One day a poet named Corpre came to King Bres's court. The poet was given pitiful quarters, a small, dark chamber without any furniture, not even a fire. Despite the hunger he felt from traveling, he received three dry cakes for his dinner and not a drop of ale to drink. The poet exacted revenge on the king with a quatrain:

"Without food quickly served,
Without a cow's milk, whereon a calf can grow,
Without a dwelling fit for a man under the gloomy night,
Without means to entertain a bardic company,
Let such be the condition of Bres."

The people of Ireland delighted in the poet's quatrain. The five lines of poetry presented the king's vices in a way that made his subjects laugh at him. The form was the first satire composed in the country. It was believed to have a magical power.

The subjects could no longer tolerate the stinginess of King Bres. In place of Bres, a new king was chosen. The king's name? He was Nuada of the Silver Hand, the rightful king of Ireland.

The Magic Cow

IRELAND

The Druids were said to have descended from heaven to earth in a cloud. The Fomorians were their worst enemies, and Balor was the name of the Fomorians' greatest king. He was called Balor "of the Evil Eye" because the gaze from his one eye wounded those who evoked his anger like a thunderbolt. At the time of this myth, Balor was very old. The eyelid that covered the evil eye drooped so heavily that the king required the assistance of several men to lift the lid with ropes. Only then could he use his killing gaze upon his enemies.

Balor received notice of a prophecy from the Druids, his enemies. The prophecy stated that the Fomorian king would be killed by his grandson. In an attempt to avoid his death, he imprisoned his only child, an infant daughter called Ethlinn, in a high tower. By Balor's decree the tower was built on a forsaken island named Tory Island. Twelve matrons were encharged with keeping Ethlinn from gazing upon a man. They were to protect her from ever learning that creatures of the opposite gender existed. As fortune would have it, Ethlinn grew into a young woman of unsurpassed beauty during her imprisonment in the tower.

Meanwhile, on the mainland there were three brothers named Kian, Sawan, and Goban the Smith. The last was the land's great maker of armor and crafted arts. Kian owned a

Upon hearing the untruth, Sawan placed the cow in the charge of the young boy.

magical cow. The cow's milk flowed so freely that everyone in the land was eager to possess her. For this reason Kian kept close watch over the animal.

One day Sawan and Kian traveled to the forge to ask Goban the Smith, their brother, to construct weapons for them. Kian carried the steel they brought for the weapons into the forge, and he appointed his brother Sawan to guard his precious cow. King Balor wanted the cow. So he changed himself into a redheaded boy. He told Sawan a lie about how he overheard the brothers decide to use all the fine steel for their swords. Sawan's sword, Balor said, would be made of base metal. Upon hearing the untruth, Sawan placed the cow in the charge of the young boy, and he hurried into the forge to confront his brothers. Seizing the opportunity, Balor stole the cow and brought her across the sea to Tory Island.

Kian discovered Balor's trickery. He enlisted the help of a Druid wise woman named Birog to take revenge on the king. Birog dressed Kian like a woman. By means of a magical spell, the wisewoman transported herself and Kian in disguise across the sea. They told the guardians of Ethlinn, Balor's imprisoned daughter, that they were two noblewomen who had been abducted to the island but they had escaped their captors. They begged entrance to the tower, and the guardians granted the request.

The wisewoman Birog cast a spell that put the guardians into a deep sleep. While they slept, Kian went to Princess Ethlinn, and he and the princess fell in love. In the morning Kian, Birog, and the magical cow were gone. Soon the guardians found that Ethlinn was pregnant. Fearful of Balor's wrath, they convinced her that her evening with Kian had been merely a dream. However, when it was time, the princess gave birth to three sons.

When Balor discovered the event, he commanded that the three babies be drowned in a whirlpool at sea. Despite the obedience of the soldier who was given the horrible duty, only two babies died. One dropped from the sheet in the soldier's grasp when a pin opened to make room for him to fall into the bay. The bay was afterward named Port na Delig, or the Haven of the Pin. It is called by that name to this day.

While his brothers drowned, the lucky baby was found by Birog and she gave the child to Kian. Kian in turn handed the baby over to Goban the Smith. Goban taught the child the fine details of his craft, and when the child grew, he was as talented an armorer and artisan as his uncle. The child was called Lugh. The Druids called him the sun god.

Lugh, the Sun God

IRELAND

Lugh, the sun god, was appointed by heaven to save his people, the Dannans, from their enemies, the Fomorians. As an infant he escaped the death sentence of the evil Fomorian king, Balor. He had been placed with his two brothers in a bundle to be drowned. But one of the pins that held the bundle together opened, and Lugh escaped. The bundle was hurled into a whirlpool at sea by King Balor's order. But Lugh had been found in the nearby bay, which was afterward named Port na Delig, or the Haven of the Pin. The bay is called the Haven of the Pin to this day.

When he was pulled from the water, Lugh was given by the wise woman Birog to his father, Kian. The child was raised by Kian's brother Goban the Smith, the armorer and craftsman. Lugh learned his uncle's arts at an early age. While he was still a youth, the Dannan elders gave him to Duach, or "The Dark" king of the Great Plain, which was also known as the Land of the Dead. Lugh lived in the Great Plain until he grew to be a man.

The myth that follows is about how Lugh fulfilled his destiny to free his people.

One day Lugh traveled to the Land of the Living. He went to the castle at Tara of the Dannan king, Nuada of the Silver Hand. The keeper of the palace asked Lugh what service he had to offer the king.

"I am a carpenter," Lugh responded.

"We have a fine carpenter now. He is called Luchta, the son of Luchad," said the keeper of the castle.

"I am also a smith," said Lugh.

"We have a master smith," answered the castle keeper.

"I'm a warrior, too," said Lugh.

"Ogma is our warrior," responded the keeper of the palace.

Lugh then told the keeper he could do a host of things. One by one he listed all the occupations and arts he knew. He was a poet, a harper, a man of science, a physician, somebody who weighed measures of things, a spencer, or on and on until he ran out of occupations. Each time Lugh offered a service to the king, the castle keeper responded as he had done the first time. That is, that the court of Nuada of the Silver Hand already had so-and-so by the name of such and such, who was a master of that particular service.

Lugh became frustrated. "Ask the king if he has one man in his service who is a master of all of these arts. If he does, then I will go away and no longer seek entrance to the castle," said Lugh proudly.

Lugh was then invited into the castle by the keeper. King Nuada of the Silver Hand granted him an audience. The king gave Lugh the surname of Ildanach, which meant "The All-Craftsman," Prince of all the Sciences. He was also given the name, Lugh Lamfada, or Lugh of the Long Arm.

When Lugh returned to the Land of the Dead, he transported many magical gifts. One was the Boat of Mananan, the son of Lir the Sea God. The boat could read a person's thoughts and could travel anywhere the person wanted to go. The second gift was the Horse of Mananan, which was able to travel to any location, by land or sea. The third object was a most powerful sword named Fragarach, or "The Answerer." Fragarach was able to penetrate the strongest armor any opponent could wear.

An assembly of Dannan chiefs gathered. When Lugh entered, he appeared to them like the rising sun on a summer's day. Under his leadership the Dannans attacked their oppressors, the Fomorians. After the fierce battle only nine Fomorians remained alive. All of the others had been slain. When the nine survivors returned to King Balor with the sad news of defeat, the Fomorian king charged his captains to mount a scorching defense. He told them to cable the island of the Dannans to their ships and to tow it to the far north region of ice and gloom. This never happened because Lugh and the Dannans prepared themselves for the final battle against the Fomorians.

Lugh would champion the fight against King Balor. The records of the time reported the ferocity of the fight: "Fearful indeed was the thunder that rolled over the battlefield; the shouts of the warriors, the breaking of the shields, the flashing and clashing of the swords, of the straight, ivory-hilted swords, the music and harmony of the 'belly-darts' and the sighing and winging of the spears and lances."

The Quest of the Sons of Turren

IRELAND

Lugh, the sun god, had a final battle to fight against King Balor and the Fomorians. The Fomorians were the enemies of Lugh's people, the Dannans. For a sure victory Lugh knew he needed to obtain certain magical objects.

Meanwhile, Lugh commissioned his father, Kian, to travel north to Ulster to rally an army of Dannans for the battle. In the vicinity of Dundalk, Kian had to cross the Plain of Murthemney. There he met three brothers, Brian, Iuchar, and Iucharba, the sons of Turenn. It happened that a blood feud existed between the houses of Turenn and Kian. So Kian changed himself into a pig to avoid recognition by the three sons of Turenn. He hurried to join the herd of pigs that was rooting, or digging, with their snouts in the dirt.

But Kian's plan was thwarted when the brothers recognized him despite the disguise. Brian cast a spear at the pig that was Kian and wounded him.

"Please, allow me to change back into a man before I am slain," begged Kian of the three sons of Turenn.

"I would rather kill a man than a pig," ridiculed Brian.

As quickly as he had become a pig, Kian was a man once again.

"Ha! I outwitted you," said Kian to the man. "Had you slain a pig, you would only have had to pay the eric, or the blood fine dictated by royal decree, for killing a pig. Now you have to pay the fine for a man. You cannot hide that it was a man, either, because the weapons you show for yourselves will tell that it was a man."

"I shall slay you with no weapons, then," retorted Brian.

The three angry brothers stoned Kian to death on the spot. Afterward they buried him deep in the ground. A short time later Lugh passed the mound of stones on the plain under which his father lay dead. The stones cried out to him about what had occurred. Lugh uncovered his father's body and vowed to take revenge on his murderers. Then he returned to Tara to the castle of the Dannan king, Nuada of the Silver Hand. When the king told Lugh to name the eric for the evil deed, Lugh told the three sons of Turenn what he required of them to make good for their crime and escape the penalty of death.

"I want only these common objects: three apples, the skin of a pig, a spear, a chariot with two horses, seven swine, a hound, a cooking spit, and, last, three shouts on a hill," demanded Lugh.

Then Lugh told the meaning of what he had asked. The three apples grew in the Garden of the Sun. The pigskin, which when laid upon the sufferer, cured every wound and sickness, belonged to the king of Greece. The spear was a magical weapon that belonged to the king of Persia. The seven swine were the possessions of King Asal of the Golden Pillars. They could be killed and eaten at night and yet be discovered unharmed the next morning. The cooking spit belonged to the sea nymphs of the sunken Island of Finchory. Lastly, the three shouts were to be yelled on the hill belonging to the fierce warrior Mochaen. The warrior and his sons had already taken a vow to stop anyone from shouting on the hill.

Despite the difficulty of their task, the sons of Turenn set out to accomplish what Lugh demanded. When they had procured all the objects but the cooking spit and had not yet shouted from the warrior's hill, Lugh made them suffer a spell of forgetfulness. The brothers returned to Tara with the magical objects they had in their possession, the very things Lugh needed to defeat the Fomorians. Then Lugh sent the brothers out once more to finish the dictates of the eric. They were unable to satisfy the final requirement of the shout without mortal injury, and they returned in need of healing. When Lugh refused them the pigskin to heal themselves, the brothers died. Their father, who had become very old, perished with them.

At the final battle between the Dannans and the Fomorians, King Nuada of the Silver Hand met King Balor. The Fomorian king, Balor, had an evil eye. He glanced upon King Nuada and several other Dannan soldiers, and they fell dead. But Lugh hurled a boulder at Balor's eye and swiftly killed him. Lugh was crowned king of the Dannans in the place of Nuada of the Silver Hand, who had been killed by the enemy king.

The Magic Cauldron

WALES

This myth is a tale about a magic cauldron. The cauldron originally came from Ireland. It resided in Wales for a time, but then it returned to Ireland. Not only did the cauldron possess certain powers, it also forged an understanding between the rulers of the two countries. Here is the story of the magic cauldron.

Bran the Blessed was king of the Isle of the Mighty, which was at the time the land of Britain and that land included Wales. Bran had his court at Harlech. At Bran's court were also the members of the royal family. These included Bran's brother Manawyddan, the son of Llyr, and his sister, Branwen. Two sons whom Bran's mother bore to Eurosswyd were also at court. Nissyen was a gentle youth. Evnissyen, by contrast, was never so content as when he caused difficulty and strife.

One day Bran looked out from Harlech at sea, and he witnessed thirteen ships sailing with the help of a fair wind from Ireland. Bright flags flew from the ships' masts. In the front ship a man held up a triangular Norman shield pointed upward in the gesture of peace. Upon landing, the visitors greeted Bran and explained the reason for their coming.

Among them was Matholwch, the king of Ireland. He had come to request the hand of Branwen, Bran's sister, in marriage. It was Matholwch's intention that the marriage forge a union between Ireland and the Isle of the Mighty, making both countries more powerful because of it.

Gaiety spread throughout the land, because Branwen was a favorite of the people. The people sang, "Branwen is the fairest damsel in the world."

Bran took counsel with his lords, then he agreed to the marriage. In the place called Aberffraw, Branwen became the bride of the Irish king. Guests feasted and celebrated in tents for many days.

During the festivities the evil Evnissyen, half brother of Bran and Branwen, chanced upon some fine horses at rest.

"To whom do these belong?" he inquired.

"They are the horses of Matholwch, Branwen's new husband," responded the keeper of the animals.

"And how has it happened that such a fine maiden as she has been given in marriage without my consent? I could be offered no greater insult," proclaimed Evnissyen.

With his words of anger, Evnissyen rushed upon the horses. He cut off their lips to the teeth, he removed the ears of their fine heads, and he chopped off their tails! He even excised the eyes of some.

When Matholwch was informed of the evildoings, he ordered his countrymen to put out to sea immediately. Bran sent messengers after the Irish king, offering sound horses for every animal that Matholwch had lost, a staff of silver as tall as himself, and a plate of gold the size of his face. Bran told his messengers to arrange a meeting between himself and Matholwch. Matholwch reluctantly agreed.

When the two kings met, Bran offered Matholwch another treasure, the magic cauldron.

"I know this cauldron," said Matholwch. "It comes from a lake in Ireland that is near the Fairy Mounds. The lake is the Lake of the Cauldron."

Matholwch told Bran a story.

"I once met a tall, ill-looking fellow with a wife bigger than himself, and the cauldron was strapped on his back," began Matholwch.

Matholwch explained that he had hired the man to work for him. Six weeks later the strange man's wife gave birth to a son, who was born as a fully armed warrior. As if the event were not odd enough, it repeated itself every six weeks. By year's end the tall, ill-looking man and his wife had so many warrior sons they could have passed as a war god and war goddess. As for the warrior sons, they fought among themselves constantly. That is, when they were not causing turmoil in the land.

Finally Matholwch had a house of iron built. He enticed the father, mother, and all their children inside. Matholwch then barred the door. He heaped coals around the house and heated them until they turned white-hot. He hoped to roast them to death. As soon as the walls softened and took on the color of the coals, the man and his wife burst through them and fled. Their warrior children remained inside and burned to death.

Bran then spoke. "The man was called Llassar Llaesgyvnewid. His wife was Kymideu Kymeinvoll. They came next to Britain," he began.

Bran explained to Matholwch that he himself had taken pity on the couple and had housed them. They filled the land with their offspring, who prospered wherever they went. Their descendants lived in strong, fortified villages and they owned the finest weapons ever seen. To repay him for his kindness, the couple gave Bran the cauldron.

Bran told the Irish king that if a slain man were thrown into the cauldron, he would emerge physically sound, but be unable to speak. Matholwch accepted the gift of the magic cauldron from Bran. Matholwch forgave Bran for his half brother's evil deed, and he sailed back to Ireland with his new wife, Branwen. Thus, a strong union was formed between the two countries.

Queen Maeve and the Wild Sow

IRELAND

Maeve was queen of Connacht. She came to life as the goddess of supreme power, or sovereignty, and no king could rule Connacht without her as queen. Maeve's kingdom was at war with the kingdom of Ulster. Both kingdoms were in Ireland.

"Queen Maeve, a hunting party has formed in the courtyard as you requested," said her groom one morning.

The queen's golden hair was tied back in a ribbon to keep it out of her way. Stout leather boots covered her feet. Her knife rested inside one of the boots next to her muscular calf. The scabbard of her sword bore her crest of a crowned wheat sprig on a field of green, red, and purple. On her shoulder was a quiver of arrows. Her crossbow was in her hands.

"Geansai," she commanded the strongest horse in the kingdom, maybe even in Ireland. His name meant jumper. He was as white as milk, and he wore the red and purple plumage of royalty.

"Huntsman, sound the charge," said Maeve, in order to begin the hunt.

Maeve was queen of Connacht.

The queen had challenged her court many times to race her for the lead. Though they had tried, not a horseman could overtake her and Geansai. Three leagues from the castle and still in the lead, Queen Maeve stopped at a crossroads. She dismounted quickly to pay respect to Flidais, goddess of the hunt. She also left an offering for Epona, the Horse Mother. Approaching hoofbeats told her the others had arrived.

"We go to the Forest of the Bottomless Cauldron today. I feel like tracking the Wild Sow of the Wilderness," she instructed the huntsman.

When the huntsman informed the rest of the court of the queen's intention, many of them asked to be excused from the hunt. The queen dismissed those that asked, because she had no use for anyone afraid of a mere pig. Only twelve warriors remained. In Maeve's eyes these were the ones worthy of the challenge. The huntsman again blew the call to the hunt, and the queen turned Geansai toward the northwest for the dense Forest of the Bottomless Cauldron.

The ground became rocky and very steep. They had to leap hedgerows on many occasions. At the crest of a tall hill, Queen Maeve paused to wait for the others. Below, the ground was lush and of the darkest green. A hint of moisture hung on the breeze. It was the Valley of the Vanished, beyond which lay the Forest of the Bottomless Cauldron. Few had survived the Forest, although Maeve had. She had gone to answer a dare once, even though the challenger had fled before entering.

"How do you wish to proceed, Queen Maeve?" asked the huntsman.

"We will go north near the stream. There we will tether the horses, as the Forest is too thick and treacherous for them," she responded.

The warriors made their way behind the queen through the density of the Forest. Silence surrounded them. The earth smelled wild. Suddenly the queen stopped in alarm. She unsheathed her sword, and the twelve warriors in her party did the same. They did not hear what she did, but they knew to trust her instincts.

A band of warriors from Ulster showed themselves in the small clearing. The boldest of them challenged Queen Maeve. He made to strike several blows, but she deflected every one of them. She assessed his battle skills and saw that before every blow he gave a hint of what his next movement would be. Thus, she was able to maneuver his back against a broad oak tree. She drew her sword, and he could not escape its thrust.

The twelve warriors in her party, meanwhile, were engaged in heavy battle with the enemy. The leader of the Ulstermen came forward.

"Who sent you? Ulster's cowardly king?" demanded Queen Maeve of the enemy leader.

When he told her no, she knew he was lying out of allegiance to the king.

"Two-thirds of your men are dead. Consider yourself lucky that I am going to allow the rest of you to escape. But you must make a promise that, if ever you return to Connacht uninvited, you will be my servant for nine years, and your firstborn will follow as my servant after you," said Maeve.

The enemy leader agreed to the sacred and magical bond she proposed. When Maeve looked to her warriors, she saw that eleven had survived despite the overwhelming number of the enemy they had fought. She sent three warriors to disarm the Ulstermen and to escort them to the border. Then she continued with the remaining eight warriors in her quest of the Wild Sow of the Wilderness.

Soon Maeve and her party came to another clearing, this one in the mouth of a dark, rounded cave. The quarry she sought rested peacefully in the mouth of the cave. The sow lowered her head and bared her teeth. She stood two heads taller than any sow the warriors had ever seen. A ring of woven silver hung from her nose. Its value was enormous, although no one in the land knew exactly how it happened to get there.

The sow made ready to charge. Several of Maeve's warriors unleashed arrows at the animal, but the sow dodged every one. The giant pig positioned its charge directly at Queen Maeve. She released a great bellow against which Maeve unloaded an arrow with her finest aim. The point lodged between the fiery eyes of the sow. The pig stumbled, righted herself, then fell dead.

Because the honor of the kill was hers, Maeve reached into her boot for her knife. She deftly cut open the sow's chest and extracted the animal's still warm heart, and she offered the prize to Flidais, goddess of the hunt.

At the castle Maeve adorned herself with the silk robes of her royal office. She was the first to taste the sow at the banquet. Her warriors received the second portions. No one in the court entertained a question about the identity of the finest warrior in the land.

Etain and Midir

IRELAND

With fifty maidens to accompany her, Etain made the short trip to a woodland pool to wash her hair. Her hair was in two golden braids. A small ball of gold hung from each. Etain sat upon the soft bank of the pool, and one of her maidens began to unfasten the long locks. Etain's reflection in the pool showed her loveliness. Her eyes were tender, and her nose and lips were perfectly sculpted. Her long neck was as delicate as a swan's.

King Eochaid of Ireland was passing through the same woods with a party of horsemen. The king and his court agreed that no one among them had ever seen such a fair maid.

"She looks to have come from the Fairy Mounds," said the king about Etain.

He began immediately to woo Etain. Shortly afterward he asked her father for Etain's hand in marriage. King Eochaid and Etain were married, and the king returned to Tara with his queen.

Strange circumstances started to show themselves. On one of the first mornings of his marriage, the king was out riding early. He was startled to find a young warrior beside him on the plain. The stranger wore a purple tunic and carried a pointed spear in one hand and a white shield speckled with gems of gold in the other. His golden hair hung to his shoulders, and his eyes were a rich gray. The king and the stranger did not exchange even a word before the warrior disappeared.

When the king returned to the castle, he informed no one in the court of what he had seen. He climbed instead to the highest tower and looked out on the plain. Upon the high ground he noticed a blossom that glowed in all the colors he had ever witnessed.

Then the king's brother Ailill fell ill. The sickness was so severe that no leech could cure it. The poor king had to leave Tara and his brother to tour his kingdom of Ireland. He begged Queen Etain to care for Ailill in his absence. He asked the queen to promise to do everything possible to cure his brother. And if Ailill were to die, the king entreated her to provide him the burial of a prince. Etain agreed to what her husband asked.

As soon as the king departed, the queen went to visit the sick Ailill to ask him what she could do to make him feel more comfortable. The prince told Etain that he was pining away out of love for her. If she did not meet him the following day outside the castle, he would surely die. Etain promised to meet Ailill because she had vowed to the king to care for his brother.

The next day Etain waited for Ailill at the meeting spot.

"You are one who has forgotten," said Ailill when he arrived. Then he left.

The following day Etain waited again.

"You are one who has forgotten," said Ailill once more before he left her alone.

On the third day Etain was also there waiting.

"O fair-haired woman, will you not come with me?" asked Ailill. And he chanted a song in her honor. When he finished, he spoke to Etain again.

"I am not Ailill. I cast him into a deep slumber, and I filled him with love for you. I am Midir the Proud, king among the Immortals. In the Land of the Immortals, I loved you. And you loved me."

Etain protested that she did not know this man who spoke to her.

He continued, nonetheless. "Fuamnach, my queen, was jealous of you. So she changed you into a butterfly. She blew a tempest, and she banished you. You flew into the palace of Oengus, the god of love, and my foster son. He made you a home of glass and put within it a garden of flowers. There he guarded you. But Fuamnach discovered your whereabouts. When you exited your glass home, she blew another tempest and drove you

She rose with Midir into the air and out of the palace window.

through the air. You traveled to the house of Etar. His wife held a drinking cup in which you landed. When she drank the ale in the cup, she swallowed you. She gave birth to you, and since that mortal birth you have forgotten me. I claim you now as my bride, queen in the Land of the Immortals."

"I am wife of the king of Ireland. I know not of your country. To me, you are a nameless man," said Etain.

"If King Eochaid gives me your hand, will you accompany me?" asked Midir.

"If he bids me, I will go," responded Etain.

When King Eochaid returned, he fleetingly saw the golden-haired stranger again on the plain. Upon entering Tara he found his brother fully cured and without any recollection of having pined for the queen. The stranger entered the castle gate after Eochaid and challenged him to a game of chess. The king accepted the challenge. They played two games, which the king won. After the first game, when the strange warrior asked the king what he desired for a prize, the king requested treasure. After the second the king asked for a great work. The stranger fulfilled both requests.

The third game began in earnest. This time around, the stranger won. For his prize he asked to hold Etain in his arms and kiss her. The king could not outrightly deny the request, as his requests had been honored. So he told the stranger to return in one month for his prize. Meanwhile, King Eochaid gathered a great army to protect the palace. At the end of the month, he hosted a marvelous feast for his nobles and his royal family. Suddenly, into the banquet hall, came Midir the Proud, whom all recognized in his true form.

"I claim my prize, King of Ireland," announced Midir.

When Midir held Etain in his arms, she remembered all the love she had felt for him in the Land of the Immortals. She rose with Midir into the air and out of the palace window. When the king and his guests hurried to look, they saw two swans in flight toward Slievenamon, Midir the Proud's fairy palace.

Branwen's Starling, Bran's Head

WALES

Branwen was the beloved sister of Bran the Blessed, king of the Isle of the Mighty, which included the land of Britain and the land of Wales. Branwen was married to Matholwch, the king of Ireland. Since her marriage Branwen lived on the island of Ireland. At the time of the marriage on the Isle of the Mighty, however, an unfortunate event took place. Bran's evil half brother destroyed the Irish king's horses. Despite the amends that were made at that time between the two kings, Bran and Matholwch, the insult remained an open wound to the Irish. The foster brothers of Matholwch fed the wound with their continued hatred of Bran. Their hatred found its way to the new Irish queen, Branwen.

On the island of Ireland, the foster brothers poisoned Matholwch's love for Branwen. The brothers influenced the king to banish his queen from the royal quarters. They made her cook for the court. They ordered the butcher to come to Branwen every day after he cut the meat and to give her a blow on the ear. Finally their hatred persuaded Matholwch to bar any passage by ship between Ireland and the Isle of the Mighty.

Poor Branwen reared a starling under cover in her kitchen. She taught the bird to speak. She told the starling how kind her brother was and of the life she used to have on the Isle of the Mighty as the good king's sister. Each day the bird grew in strength. One day Branwen attached a letter she wrote about her woes in Ireland to the bird's wing. Then she sent the starling to her brother. The loyal bird found Bran and lighted upon his shoulder, ruffling its feathers so the king could see the letter.

After he read it, the grieving Bran called together sevenscore and four of his chief-men, a total of 144 loyal followers. They met together in council and decided to rescue Branwen. They set sail immediately.

Some swineherds were upon the beach in Matholwch's kingdom. "Lord, we have marvelous news," they told their king. "A wood we have seen upon the sea. Beside the wood was a vast mountain that moved. A lofty ridge was at the top of the mountain, and a lake was on either side of the ridge. And the wood and the mountain, and the ridge and the lake, all these things moved," they exclaimed.

"There is none who can know anything concerning this but Branwen," responded King Matholwch.

When asked to explain, Branwen's heart jumped. "The trees of the forest are the yards and masts of the sea. The mountain is Bran, my brother. The ridge is his nose that pulsates with wrath. His two eyes are the lakes on either side of the ridge."

The men of the island of Ireland entered Matholwch's palace from one side. The men of the Isle of the Mighty came by the other direction. They sat together in council, and there was peace between them. King Bran called the boy Nissyen, son of Branwen, and the future king of Ireland, to himself. Nissyen then went forward to Bran's evil half brother, the same half brother who had destroyed the horses that belonged to Matholwch. At that instant the half brother cried out, knowing the unthinkable deed he was about to do. He took hold of Nissyen and threw him into the fire, where he burned to death.

Bran grasped his sister with one hand and his shield with his other. He supported Branwen between the shield and his shoulder during the terrible fight that followed. Only seven of the warriors from the Isle of the Mighty survived. King Bran himself was wounded in the foot with a poison dart. He commanded his warriors to cut off his head and carry it to the White Tower in London, under which they were to bury it with his face toward France.

Branwen cried out, "Woe is me that I was ever born. Two islands have been destroyed because of me."

She uttered a piercing moan, and her heart broke. Her countrymen buried her on the island of Ireland upon the banks of the Alaw. The evil half brother of Bran threw himself into the fire where the prince had burned. And his heart burst open, too.

The seven survivors from the Isle of the Mighty set sail, bearing Bran's mighty head. They buried it as he had directed them. Bran intended the head to lie under the White Tower as a charm against invasion.

Caradoc, Bran's son, when told of his father's death, also died of a broken heart. Caswallawn, a son of Beli, had grabbed the throne of Bran and the other sons of Llyr while Bran was on the island of Ireland. He began to rule as king of the Isle of the Mighty.

READ-ALOUD MYTHS AND LEGENDS

Scandinavian Myths

Fire and Ice: The Beginning of the World

In the beginning of time, nothing existed except for Allfather. Allfather was a powerful entity that was unseen and unheard. There was no light, no earth, no seas, no birds or animals, no humans. There was darkness everywhere.

In the great void of the universe, there was a chasm so deep and dark that it was impossible to guess how far down it descended. It was called the chasm of yawning, or Ginnungagap. To the north of the chasm was Niflheim, a great area of mist that rose above the flowing streams of the Elivagar. The streams and mist eventually found their way to the yawning chasm, where they delivered their waters to the hungry mouth of rock. When the cold air of the chasm touched the water, it caused it to turn to ice. Soon the chasm was covered with a glistening frozen waterfall.

To the south of this region was the land of Muspellheim. It was here that the element of fire existed, jealously guarded by Surtr, the flame giant. Surtr possessed a magnificent light sword that flashed through the darkness of the universe, and sent sparks flying everywhere. Several embers fell into the chasm of ice, melting some of the frozen waters.

Great clouds of steam rose above the abyss, then cooled. Layer upon layer of frost appeared as the heat and the cold came together. From this union, through the will of Allfather, Ymir, an ice giant, was created.

Ymir stumbled through the rocky landscape. He was hungry. Eventually he found a giant cow whose udder was dripping with sweet milk. Ymir knew that this creature, called Audhumla, was fashioned from the same forces that had created him. He approached the cow and asked permission to drink her milk. The cow consented.

While Ymir was busy drinking Audhumla's milk, the great cow began to lick an ice block with her tongue in hopes of finding salt. Over and over her large cow's tongue stripped away layers of the ice; until at last a figure began to appear in the transparent block.

The creature was known as the god Buri.

Meanwhile, Ymir, who was now greatly satisfied by his meal of cow's milk, fell asleep on the ground. While he slept, two children appeared from under his arm. One was a girl and the other a boy. A giant with six heads sprang from his immense feet. The giant was called Thrudgelmir, and he immediately had a son, whom he called Bergelmir.

Buri, who had come from the ice, also had children. His children had children and thus, an entire race of gods and goddesses was created. The giants felt threatened by these creatures and decided to attack them. A war began that would last many, many years. It was the war between the ice, or frost, giants and the gods and goddesses.

Finally Buri's son Bor married the giantess Bestla. Together they had three children: Odin, or "spirit," Vili, or "will," and Ve, or "holy." The three sons of Buri and Bestla joined in the war against the frost giants. They killed the great giant Ymir. Ymir was so big that his blood flooded the world, drowning all the other giants except for his grandson, Bergelmir. Bergelmir and his wife managed to escape from the deluge of blood and retreated to a place known as Jotunheim, or the home of the giants. Here they existed for many, many years and produced numerous offspring, who would begin a new race of frost giants.

The gods and goddesses, meanwhile, decided to use the enormous corpse of the giant Ymir. From his flesh they created the earth, or Midgard. From his blood and sweat, they created the oceans, rivers, and streams. His teeth became cliffs and mountains; his hair became trees, bushes, and vegetation.

Ymir's great skull was raised high above the newly created earth and formed the foundation for heaven. His brains drifted through the expanse of sky and became clouds. Four dwarfs were positioned beneath the skull to hold it in place. They were called North, South, East, and West. Inside the skull the gods and goddesses trapped bits of sparks from the sword of Surtr, which became stars and comets. From the larger embers they fashioned the sun and moon.

The sun, Sol, and moon, Mani, traveled through the sky in glorious chariots drawn by powerful horses. They were surrounded by beings known as Dawn, Day, Noon, Afternoon, Night, and the Four Seasons. Thus, the new world became logical and organized.

The chariots of Sol and Mani were chased through the sky by two fierce wolves called Skoll, or "repulsion," and Hati, "hatred." The wolves hoped to capture the two celestial beings and eat them so that the earth could return to perpetual darkness once more. The inhabitants of the earth, however, carefully watched the skies for the presence of the wolves, and when they saw them, they made such noise that they scared them away.

Other creatures sprang from the decaying corpse of Ymir. These beings were known as dwarfs, trolls, or gnomes. The gods and goddesses endowed these creatures with great intelligence, but soon discovered that they had a very mischievous nature. Eventually the dwarfs were banished to the underworld, where they were forced to remain during the day. There they mined for precious metals like gold and silver.

Some of the small creatures that came from Ymir were not evil. They were known as fairies or elves, and were permitted to live in the skies.

The god Odin, who had been the leader of all the other gods and goddesses, found a special place for them to dwell, known as Asgard. It was here that the twelve gods and twenty-four goddesses lived and ruled over the universe.

Odin and the Wall

Odin was the most powerful and revered of all the Norse gods and goddesses. He was the son of Bor and Bestla, who also produced two other sons, Vili and Ve. It was Odin who organized the Norse deities in the great kingdom of Asgard, dispensing his wisdom, judgment, and passion for battle. Odin sat upon his throne wearing a blue mantle, or cloak, around his shoulders. He held the spear Gungnir at his side while he was at court. Gungnir was so powerful that anyone who took an oath before it could never break his promise. On his finger he wore the powerful ring known as Draupnir. It was made of gold and covered with precious stones.

Odin was known to wander the earth of Midgard in disguise. He dressed as an old man with a cane, a floppy, brimmed hat, and gray hair. He only had one eye, for he had sacrificed the other in order to gain all of the wisdom contained in the well of Mimir, the giant. Odin was greatly interested in the events of Midgard. He had two ravens, Huginn ("thought") and Muninn ("memory"), who flew around the earth by day, and returned to tell Odin all they had seen and heard each night.

Odin was constantly aware of the danger of the frost giants, fierce-looking creatures who lived in the land of Jutunheim. The gods and goddesses of Asgard had been battling with the giants for many years. One day a stranger approached Odin with a suggestion of how to protect Asgard from an attack.

"Great Odin," the stranger began, "I can build a wall that can go around the land of

Odin was the most powerful and revered of all the Norse gods and goddesses.

the gods and goddesses. This wall will be so high and so thick that no one will be able to penetrate it."

Odin was intrigued by the stranger's plan. But he was wise enough to know that such a project would cost a great deal. He asked the stranger what payment he expected in return for such a wall.

"I will tell you, soon," the stranger told Odin. "There is much work to do. I will have your wall built within a year."

Odin thought for a moment. A wall to keep out the frost giants would be worth any cost, provided that the stranger would complete the wall in one year's time. He decided that he would allow the stranger to begin.

The stranger left Asgard and returned the following morning. He brought with him a strong, large horse. Everyone expected that the horse would be used to pull stones to the site of the wall. Amazingly, it was the horse who lifted the stones to their respective positions, and then applied mortar to them to keep them in place. The horse worked both day and night without stopping for food or water.

The gods and goddesses of Asgard watched in wonder as the wall took shape. It grew higher and higher with every passing day. Odin was also awed at this achievement. Yet, in his heart, he was fearful of the price the stranger might extract for such a feat.

Odin approached the stranger again.

"We are grateful for your hard work," he told him. "But, we are anxious to know what it is that you expect for payment."

The stranger answered Odin.

"When I have completed the wall, as I have agreed, you must give me the sun, the moon, and the goddess Freyja."

Amazingly, it was the horse who lifted the stones to their respective positions, and then applied mortar to them to keep them in place.

Odin was horrified when he heard the stranger's request.

"I cannot give you these things!" he replied. "No one can own the sun and the moon, for the world will die without them. And, I am not willing to give you the goddess Freyja."

"Then, I cannot continue my work," the stranger told him.

The stranger and his horse left Asgard. The wall was unfinished. Odin was in despair until the figure of Loki appeared before him. Loki was a being who was half god, half creature, for his father was the wind giant.

"I can help you," Loki told Odin. "Let the stranger continue to build the wall. I promise you that he will not finish in the time he has promised. Then, you do not have to give him what he asks for."

Odin summoned the stranger back to Asgard and told him to continue his work. He promised him that if he did complete the wall within a year, he would give him the sun and the moon and the goddess Freyja.

The stranger and the horse resumed their frantic pace and continued to build the wall. Again, day after day, the stones rose higher and higher around Asgard.

One evening, shortly before the year's deadline would arrive, Loki turned himself into a white female horse. In this form he approached the wall. He pranced in the moonlight before the stranger's horse, Svadilfari. Svadilfari had never seen such a beautiful creature. With little coaxing he forgot what he had been doing and followed the mare into the woods.

The next morning the stranger arrived at the work site to find that his helper, the horse, was missing. He searched for Svadilfari high and low, but he could not find him. Angered and shamed, he knew that he could not complete the wall in time. He left Asgard.

The rest of the gods and goddesses completed the unfinished section of the wall. They were happy in knowing that they were protected from the frost giants. Odin, however, was not as pleased. He was saddened that he had tricked the stranger. In his heart he knew that one day the stranger would seek revenge and side with the frost giants in a terrible war.

The Hammer of Thor

When great dark clouds appear over the lands in the North, and the rumbling of thunder can be heard on distant hills, the people sometimes remark that the clamor they hear is the approaching sound of the god Thor.

The Norsemen revered and worshipped Thor for his many powers and attributes. The red-haired son of the god Odin and his wife Erda was tall and strong and muscular. He was an imposing figure in the face of his enemies.

Thor lived in Asgard, the home of the gods and goddesses in the great palace called Bilskirnir, or lightning. His association with lightning probably came from the time he spent with the gods Vingnir and Hlora, who represented "wings" and "heat." Thor's palace contained 540 rooms, where he entertained his guests with lavish entertainment and wonderful food.

Thor possessed the mighty hammer Miolnir, or "the crusher." He would throw his hammer at the frost giants in battle and send them running in fear. No matter how far Thor threw his hammer, it would always return to his hand. Miolnir blazed with sparks of fire. It was said that Thor was not permitted to cross the rainbow into Asgard with the hammer in his hand, for fear it would melt the beautiful ice bridge.

No matter how far Thor threw his hammer, it would always return to his hand.

"I am the Thunderer! Here in my Northland,
My fastness and fortress, Reign I forever,
Here amid icebergs, rule I the nations;
This is my hammer, Miolnir the mighty;
Giants and sorcerers cannot withstand it."

SAGA OF KING OLAF (Longfellow)

The Norse considered Miolnir a sacred object, not only of battle, but of blessing. Just as Christians make the sign of the cross, the ancient Norse would cross themselves to make the sign of the "hammer." This symbolic gesture was also used to bless a newborn infant or a newly married couple, and to bid a final farewell to a corpse on a funeral pyre.

The countries of the North portrayed Thor in different ways. In Sweden he was depicted wearing a broad-rimmed, floppy hat. Some believed that the roar of thunder during a storm was the sound of his chariot wheels rolling across the firmament of heaven. Others, like the German people, believed the noise came from the pots and kettles he tied to the sides of the chariot.

Thor often traveled to Jotunheim, the land of the giants. The frost giants were badly behaved and thought nothing of provoking the gods and goddesses by sending frozen blasts of air into the world and destroying all vegetation and crops. During one journey to subdue the giants, Thor and Loki came upon a valley shrouded in mist. It was difficult to see anything around them. Stepping carefully through the fog, they found a peculiar dwelling that resembled a cave. Tired from their long journey, they decided to rest inside the mouth of the cave until morning.

Imagine their surprise when they woke up the next morning and discovered that they had been sleeping in a frost giant's glove! Fortunately, the giant was not malicious and agreed to guide Thor and Loki to the great palatial fort in the land of the giants.

When they arrived at the fort, Thor addressed the king of the frost giants, who was Utgard-Loki. He told the king that he had come to do battle with the giants, if necessary, to prevent them from troubling the gods and goddesses of Asgard.

Utgard-Loki was slightly amused at Thor's speech.

"I propose a contest," he told Thor. "Then, we can avoid battle with the mighty Thor and his hammer."

Thor thought for a moment, and then agreed.

"The first contest will be to see who can eat the most—a god or a giant," Utgard-Loki said.

Loki eagerly stepped up to the challenge.

"I'm so hungry," he declared. "There is no one who can eat more than I can."

The king called for a table to be piled with all kinds of meat. Then he summoned his cook from the kitchen and told him to sit at one end of the table while Loki sat at the other. He gave them the signal to begin eating.

Loki devoured the meat in no time. But to his dismay, the cook had not only eaten the meat, but the wooden table as well!

The next contest involved drinking. Utgard-Loki filled an enormous ram's horn with broth and brought it before Thor.

"If you can drink the entire contents of this horn in less than three gulps, you will win," he told him.

Thor placed the horn to his lips and drank as much as he could. However, no matter how hard he tried, he could not empty the horn. Reluctantly he conceded defeat.

Loki was instructed to run a race with a giant named Hugi. Hugi beat Loki without making any effort.

Thor was next challenged to lift Utgard-Loki's cat, who weighed a great deal. Thor felt confident that he could perform this deed with little problem. After struggling for many minutes, however, he was only able to raise the cat's paw off the ground.

Utgard-Loki smiled at the pair of gods.

"It seems to me that you have lost the contest," he told them.

"Apparently, we have," Thor said angrily.

Then Utgard-Loki shook his head and laughed out loud.

"Mighty Thor," he began. "I was warned of your arrival by one of the giants. Knowing that you were coming, and that you were a fierce warrior, I created these challenges to be unfair. Loki's challenger in the eating contest was none other than Logi, or wild fire. He ran his race with Thialfi, the fastest runner in the universe. When you attempted to drink from the horn, you were unaware that the bottom of the vessel was connected to the sea, and would be replenished with liquid after every swallow. Even the cat you attempted to lift was none other than the serpent who circles Midgard and is anchored deep into the soil of the earth. So, you see, no one could have won these contests!"

Thor was deeply angered by the frost giant's deception. He took out his hammer and attempted to throw it at the walls of the king's palace, but a great fog covered everything and made it impossible to see.

Thor and Loki left the world of the frost giants, knowing they had not completed their mission. They knew, however, that many more occasions would arise to do battle with the cunning giants in the future.

Seven Hundred Rings—Volund and the Valkyries

The Valkyries

Young, beautiful, courageous, and kind—these were some of the attributes of the Valkyries, the personal attendants of Odin. These battle maidens, who were the children of mortal kings or gods, served the all-powerful Odin by guiding the worthy souls of soldiers from the fields of combat into the afterlife of Valhalla.

The young women rode on magnificent white steeds that resembled clouds at sunrise. Garbed in helmets of silver and gold, with shields and spears flashing, they rode into battle and bestowed upon the wounded a gentle kiss that signified the beginning of the warrior's journey to heaven. Once they were in the kingdom of Valhalla, the soldiers were comforted by the Valkyries, who fed them nourishing food and filled their vessels with thirst-quenching mead, or ale.

Occasionally the maidens of Odin liked to travel to the earth to enjoy themselves and rest. To make such a journey, they donned the plumage of swans—brilliant, white feathers that covered their bodies. Once on earth they searched for a cool stream or small river in which to bathe. They left their swan's plumage on the banks of the water, and delighted in swimming in the warm sunshine.

It was not uncommon for mortals to spot the Valkyries while they were bathing. If one so desired, it was possible to prevent the maidens from leaving the earth by stealing their swan costumes. This happened one day to three Valkyries, Olrun, Alvit, and Svanhvit. Three young and handsome brothers were walking through the woods when they spied the women in a stream. Quietly they approached them through the bushes and took their swans' feathers. The maidens had no choice but to remain with the brothers. Thus, they stayed on the earth for many years and behaved as mortal wives. The story even claims that the women fell deeply in love with the brothers.

After a time, however, the maidens longed to return to Odin. They found their swans' plumage, which had been hidden in the woods, and took off from the land. When the brothers discovered what had happened, they were heartbroken. Two of the brothers decided to venture out to find their wives. The third brother, Volund, decided to remain behind, believing that one day his wife would remember their love and return to him. As a master craftsman, he enjoyed creating remarkable ornaments. Out of sorrow he spent his days re-creating the ring his beloved bride had given to him. Volund made seven hundred copies of the ring. He never tired of the work.

When he returned home from a day in the village, he sat and admired his rings. One day, to his surprise, he discovered that one ring was missing. His heart was full of hope that perhaps his wife had left him a sign that one day she would return.

That night, while he was sleeping, the soldiers of King Nidud of Sweden came upon Volund and took him as a captive. They took away his rings and the magical sword that he had forged. Knowing that Volund was a master smith, King Nidud forced him to create weapons and ornaments for his palace. Thus Volund worked like a slave for many, many years.

Garbed in helmets of silver and gold, with shields and spears flashing, they rode into battle and bestowed upon the wounded a gentle kiss.

Volund dreamed of being reunited with his wife. In hopes of escaping from the cruel king, he fashioned a pair of wings that resembled the ones his wife possessed. He kept them hidden from the watch guards in the palace as he continued his work.

A perfect opportunity for Volund to obtain his freedom finally presented itself. The king wished to have Volund's magical sword repaired. He took it to the imprisoned smith. Volund cleverly replaced his sword with another sword he had created. Taking his long-lost weapon in his hands, he was able to slay the prison guards. Before leaving the palace, however, he made the guards' skulls and teeth into jewelry, which he sent to the royal family as a tribute. Volund strapped on the wings he had created and flew past the window of the king. He called out to King Nidud and taunted him.

The king dispatched an archer to try and shoot Volund out of the sky. But the archer's arrow only managed to pierce a small sack of blood that Volund carried beneath his wing. Thinking that Volund was mortally wounded, the king praised his archer.

Volund flew far away from the king's palace and back to his small cottage. There, much to his surprise, he found his wife asleep in a chair. On her finger was the ring she had taken from his workshop. Filled with joy and happiness, Volund picked up the sleeping woman in his arms and flew with her to Alfheim, where they lived together in peace and harmony with the gods and goddesses.

Ragnarok–Winter of the World

Winter over Jotunheim

The end of the world that the Norse god Odin had predicted would come was called Ragnarok. It was the great battle between the gods and goddesses and their enemies, the frost giants.

For three long years the season of winter fell over Jotunheim, the sacred tree of the world. The first year, a heavy blanket of snow covered the lands and seas. A cruel, cold wind blew constantly, day and night, without ceasing. It was difficult for humans to keep warm. There was no spring for the planting of crops, and no autumn for harvesting them.

During the second year, the winter of the sword, there was much fighting in the world. The battlefields were filled with corpses; families fought against each other for food and supplies. Human blood stained the ever drifting white snow.

The third year of winter was known as the winter of the wolf. An evil witch fed the great wolf Managarm on the bodies of those who were slain in battle. Managarm's appetite was insatiable. The more flesh he tasted, the more he wanted. The gods and goddesses of Asgard trembled as they thought of the prophecy they knew would come true. One day a ferocious wolf would spring from the bowels of the earth and eat the sun and moon, and the world would be no more.

In the depths of Hel, the underworld, a red rooster crowed. It woke the sleeping frost giants and stirred them to action. In the realm of the gods and goddesses, a golden cock announced the arrival of the greatest battle of all: Ragnarok.

Meanwhile, another wolf, Fenrir, pulled on the magic cord that bound him to the icy side of a mountain. He hungered for the opportunity to join the forces of Hel and the frost giants and to fight against the Aesir, the immortal gods. It was common knowledge that Fenrir could crush the universe with his jaws.

The armies of the Aesir mounted their horses and began the journey to combat the forces of the evil frost giants. Their numbers were so great that the world shook from the vibrations of the horses' hooves on the icy paths of the earth.

The venomous serpent Midgardsorm, who had been sleeping at the bottom of the seas, rose from the waves in a terrible rush of water. Great waves sprung into the air, bringing tidal waves and destruction to the earth. All living mortals were washed away. As the waters of the sea covered everything in sight, the frost giants climbed aboard their ship Naglfar, and joined the ships from the underworld.

Two mighty armies were about to converge in the middle of the universe. Before the cave of Gnipa, a hound howled in the winter winds. His wails announced the terrible event about to occur.

The god Odin retreated to the well of Mimir, to consult with the head of the giant. He dipped his hands into the well of wisdom and asked Mimir what he should do as the leader of all gods and goddesses.

Mimir advised Odin to take the Aesir to Vigrith, crossing over the rainbow bridge,

Bifrost, that separated the world of the gods from the world of the frost giants. There, a decisive battle for control of the universe would be fought.

The frost giants had already reached the bridge. They attempted to cross it, in their great numbers, but the bridge could not support them. It gave way, spilling the giants into the valley below.

When the forces of gods and goddesses reached Bifrost, they saw that it had been destroyed, and they led their horses down the steep slopes of the valley to the bottom.

By now all the armies were gathered. The battleships of Hel with their gleaming blood-red sails joined the dark ship of the frost giants. The wolf Fenrir had broken free of his bonds and leaped into the fray. Down the ragged sides of the valley rode Odin and Thor, Freyja and Frey, and all the other gods and goddesses. They were joined by the fallen heroes of Valhalla.

Odin turned toward the legions behind him and spoke. "It is here that we must fight for control of the world. If we must die, let us die so that the forces of Hel and the frost giants are destroyed forever, and the world will know peace once more."

With that, he rode into battle. The wolf Fenrir spotted him and opened his mighty jaws wide enough to devour Odin. The mighty god was no more.

Thor rushed to seek revenge for Odin's death but was stopped by the serpent Midgardsorm. Midgardsorm opened his mouth, about to spray the world with a film of deadly poison. But Thor took his hammer, Miolnir, and struck the huge snake nine times. Midgardsorm reared his ugly head one last time before he exhaled enough venom to kill Thor.

One by one the gods and goddesses of the Aesir fell to the deadly forces that surrounded them. The trickster Loki killed the guardian of the rainbow bridge, Heimdall. The god Tyr managed to defend himself valiantly through the battle, until the hound of Hel caught him by surprise and fatally attacked him.

Fires blazed everywhere, consuming the trunk and branches of Yggdrasil. The great eagle, perched in the highest branches of the tree, screeched before flying away in the heavens. Finally Sol and Mani, the sun and earth, were devoured by wolves, and the universe fell into darkness once more.

When the battle of Ragnarok was over, a calm silence fell over the smoking remains of the world. From the ashes of the destruction, the sons of Odin, Vidar and Vali, and the sons of Thor, Modi and Magni, rose up and climbed to the top of a mountain. There they found the hammer of the slain god Thor and used its magical powers to destroy the remaining forces of the frost giants.

In time, as Odin had claimed, the world returned to its former beauty. The four seasons returned; a new sun and a new moon were born. Lif and Lifthrasir, a man and a woman who had survived the great flood of the deadly serpent, walked along the face of the earth and began a new race of people that survive to this day.

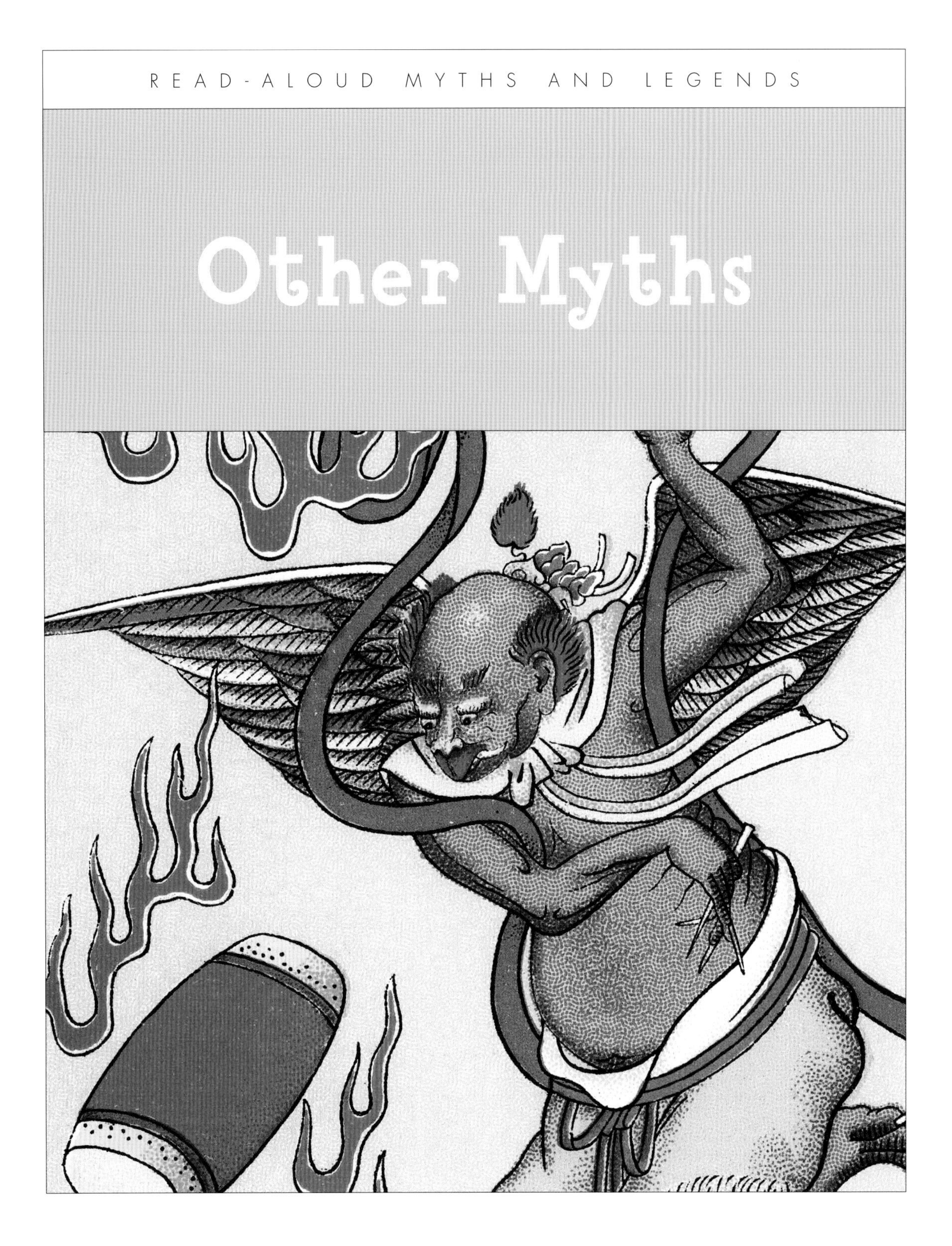
READ-ALOUD MYTHS AND LEGENDS
Other Myths

How the Sun and the World Were Created

EGYPT

In the beginning the world was a waste of water where the Great Father lived. Nu was the name of the water and of the Great Father, because the water and the god were deep. The sun god appeared as a shining egg that floated upon Nu's breast.

Ra is the name by which the sun god is best known. Ra was greater than Nu. He became the divine father and ruler of all the gods. The first gods he created were Shu, the god of wind and air, who wore an ostrich feather on his head, and his twin sister, Tefnut, who had the head of a lioness. Tefnut was the goddess of the dew and the rain. Their children were Geb and Nut.

Ra had commanded Geb and Nut not to have children. They were to remain childless every month of the year. But the god Thoth, who was guardian of the moon, took pity on the pair. Thoth created five new days, which, before then, had not belonged to

Isis waited anxiously for the secret name of Ra. Then she felt it in her heart.

the Egyptian calendar of three hundred days. On the five new days Geb and Nut gave birth to five children, including Osiris, Isis, and Nephthys.

Upon Ra's orders Shu forever separated Geb, the earth god, from Nut, the goddess of the sky. Shu elevated Nut into the air and held her belly in the sky with his arms. Only her toes and fingertips touched the earth. Across Nut's belly were the stars and the constellations, which formed the arch of the heavens in Shu's arms and which lighted the earth.

Ra had a secret name, which neither the gods nor men knew. The goddess Isis, daughter of the earth and the sky, and great-granddaughter of Ra, wanted to know the name. But Ra hid his name in his heart and would not reveal it through speech.

Ra had grown very old, and he drooled when he spoke. One day Isis followed the sun god as he walked on the earth. Looking closely at the ground, she found saliva that had dripped from Ra's mouth. With her power of enchantment Isis baked the saliva along with some particles of the earth upon which it lay. She shaped the mixture into an invisible, venomous serpent. When Ra came near the serpent, it stung him. The sun god was stricken with pain so unbearable that the cry that broke from his lips was heard in highest heaven.

His body trembled and his teeth clattered. The venom overflowed his flesh like the Nile River when it flooded the land of Egypt. Finally the ancient god calmed his affliction enough to speak.

"Gather about me, you who are my children, so that I may make known the grievous thing that has befallen me. I am stricken with great pain, so great that never before has such sorrow and pain been mine. Lo! I have not the power to make known who has stricken me thus," said Ra.

All of Ra's children grieved with the sun god except Isis, who spoke, "Reveal your secret name, divine Father, for its power must surely deliver you from your pain and distress."

But Ra cried out once more only in pain. Poison burned his flesh. His body trembled. He appeared on the verge of death.

Again Isis spoke to him. "If you will reveal your name of power to me, I will have the strength to heal you."

In his pain Ra raged, "It is my will that Isis be given my secret name, that it leave my heart and enter hers."

When he had spoken these words, Ra vanished for a short time from the eyes of the other gods. Thick darkness covered the earth. Isis waited anxiously for the secret name of Ra. Then she felt it in her heart.

"Depart, O venom, from Ra. Come forth from his heart and his flesh, flow out from his mouth. Let Ra live, for the secret name has been given to me," said Isis.

The words of Isis healed the sun god, who was made whole again. Yet, Ra was indeed old, and in a short time other gods would question his rule as Isis did. The ingratitude of humans finally drove Ra far into the heavens beyond reach. At that time Nut, the goddess of the sky, took the form of a cow and carried Ra on her back into the vault of heaven.

Isis and Osiris

EGYPT

Isis and Osiris were the daughter and son of Geb, the earth god, and Nut, the goddess of the sky. Set was their younger brother, who was very jealous of Osiris. The struggle between Osiris and Set is one of the best-known myths of ancient Egypt. Out of their struggle, Osiris became known for all things related to creation, the water of life, and blessing. Set became the symbol of destruction, drought, and evil.

When Osiris was born, a voice from within the heavens proclaimed, "Now has come the lord of all things."

The prophecy was true. When the sun god and creator, Ra, ascended into heaven on the back of Nut, who had taken the form of a cow, Osiris took Ra's place. He became king of the gods and the land of Egypt. Under the rule of Osiris, peace prevailed over all of Egypt.

Osiris was king, and Isis was queen. Isis possessed great wisdom. When humankind required food to eat, Isis gathered wild barley and wheat. With the gift from Isis, Osiris taught humans to till the soil, which had been flooded, to sow seed, and to reap the harvest. Osiris saw that peace and prosperity thrived in Egypt, so he set out to teach this wisdom to all humans. Isis reigned over Egypt in the absence of Osiris.

Then, to wondrous applause, Osiris came forward.

But in the absence of Osiris, Set determined to stir up rebellion in Egypt. At his every turn, however, Isis was stronger, and she thwarted Set's efforts. Set then plotted outright against Osiris. In his camp were seventy-two men and the queen of Ethiopia.

A great feast was held in Egypt upon the return of Osiris. Set attended with his fellow conspirators. He also brought a decorated chest made in the measurements of the body of Osiris, the king of the land. Amid the joyous celebration of the feast, Set announced that he would bestow the chest upon the person whose body fit the box's exact proportions. One after another, the guests tried to enter the chest, but to no avail. Then, to wondrous applause, Osiris came forward. He lay down and filled the box in its every dimension. When he went to raise himself in triumph, the evil conspirators sprang forward and shut the lid. They nailed it fast and sealed it with lead.

Within the rampant confusion that followed, Set commanded his evil followers to secretly dispose of the chest in the Nile River. When morning came, Osiris, still inside the chest, was carried out to the ocean. The chest and its occupant tossed hopelessly upon the waves.

Grief stricken, Isis donned the garments of mourning and wandered the land of Egypt, searching for the body of Osiris. She roamed long days in vain until she came upon some children by the shore. They told her how the chest had entered the sea at the mouth of the Nile. Meanwhile, the traitor Set ascended to the throne of Osiris.

Isis became a fugitive in the kingdom, where she sought protection from her enemies and those of the former king. Seven scorpions served as her protectors. Watching from heaven, Ra witnessed her distress, and he took pity.

One day Isis came to the house of a poor woman. But upon seeing the scorpions, the woman slammed the door. One scorpion found entry into the house. The scorpion bit the woman's child, and the unfortunate child died. The poor mother shrieked with sorrow, which touched the heart of Isis. The queen uttered some magical words, and the dead child came back to life. Accepting the woman's invitation, Isis remained in the house, where she gave birth to her son, Horus.

Word of the birth of Horus reached Set, who became determined to put the infant to death. Out of heaven, to the rescue of the rightful heir to the throne of Osiris, came the god Thoth. Thoth warned Isis of the danger, and she fled with Horus into the night.

Thoth, the moon guardian, had the head of an ibis, a bird like a heron except with a long, downwardly curved bill. Above the ibis was a moon disc. Thoth possessed complete wisdom. He invented the arts and the sciences. He measured time and was charged with all the calculations. At times Thoth was as powerful as Ra, the sun god and creator.

Because of Thoth, Horus would grow into manhood, and one day he would slay the murderer of his father.

The Ebony Horse

ARABIA

The ebony horse is one story from a great collection of tales known as *The Thousand and One Nights*, or *The Arabian Nights*. These stories may have originated in North Africa, though some have been traced to Persia and ancient India. They were told in the marketplaces of the Moslem world during the Middle Ages.

The story begins with Sabur, the king of the Persians, who was a wealthy, powerful man. Sabur was respected by those he ruled, for he was kind, compassionate, and fair. He had three beautiful daughters who were compared to the stars in the heavens and the fragrant blossoms of the garden. Sabur also had a son, the prince Kamar al-Akmar, or Moon of Moons.

One day three men came to Sabur's kingdom with the intent of offering him gifts. The first man was Hindi, or Indian; the second was a Greek; and the third was a Farsi, or Persian.

The Hindi presented Sabur with a golden horn.

The king then asked the man what was the purpose of his gift.

"This horn shall warn you, Sire, if enemies approach your city."

The king was pleased with the gift and took it gratefully.

He brought before him a magnificent wooden horse carved of fine ebony.

The Greek offered Sabur a basin of silver in which rested a peacock of gold and twenty-four chicks.

"How can I use this gift?" the king asked.

"The golden peacock will peck one of each of its chicks on the hour, for twenty-four hours, thus allowing you to tell what time it is."

The king was also delighted with this present.

Next the Persian approached the king. He brought before him a magnificent wooden horse carved of fine ebony.

"This is a beautiful statue, my friend," the king declared. "How does it work?"

"Sire," the Persian replied, "this horse has the ability to fly through the air and to take you wherever you wish to go. Let me demonstrate."

With that, the man climbed upon the wooden horse and turned a key in the horse's neck. Magically, the animal's hooves left the ground and it glided with its rider throughout the palace hall. The king was overcome with awe.

"I am so pleased with my gifts," the king announced. "I wish to give to you three something in return. Is there anything that you wish for?"

The three consulted with each other and then spoke.

"We would like the hands of your fair daughters in marriage," they told him.

"Consider it done," the king replied.

The king's daughters were in hiding while this conversation was taking place and had heard what was about to transpire. The two older princesses were not entirely displeased with the arrangement, but the youngest princess knew that she was the most beautiful, and that her father would give her to the man who had presented him with the most fascinating gift. This would be the Persian, and his ugliness and old age caused the young girl to shudder.

She retreated to her room and began to cry. Meanwhile, her brother, the prince, was passing by and heard her wailing.

"What is the matter, dear Sister?" he asked her.

"Our father has promised me in marriage to an old, ugly man."

"Don't fear," the prince assured his sister. "Let me handle this situation."

Kamar al-Akmar went to his father and told him that he was not impressed with the Persian's flying horse, and less impressed with the idea that the princess should marry such a man.

"Don't judge him, yet" the king advised his son. "Take a ride on the ebony horse, and perhaps you will change your mind."

The prince agreed to do this and mounted the wooden steed. The Persian, fearing that the prince's opinion would influence the king, decided to play a trick on him.

"Here is the key to make the horse climb into the sky," he told the prince. "Happy journeys to you, Your Majesty."

The prince turned the key, and the horse rose from the palace floor. It rose higher and higher until the ceiling could not contain it. It broke through one of the skylights and continued to climb into the air.

The prince, however, was wise enough to know what the Persian had done. "This man is trying to get rid of me so that he may have my sister. If there is a key to make this animal climb into the air, then there must be a key to make it descend, as well."

The prince felt along the horse's neck, and sure enough, he found another key, which he turned. The horse began to descend. Thrilled by his discovery, the prince took the horse over many lands, rising and diving at will to see the wonders of the world.

He happened upon a great palace, like the palace of his father. He guided the ebony horse to the roof and looked inside one of the windows. There, to his surprise, he found a woman sleeping alone. She was the most beautiful woman he had ever seen. He walked over to her, but not before the guards of the palace were upon him.

"You will die, intruder," they told him. "Come with us before this lady's father and state your case."

The prince went before the sultan of the palace and tried to explain that he was of royalty, as well, and wished to marry the sleeping princess.

"If this is true," the sultan declared, "you must demonstrate your worthiness to all of us. You must enter into battle with my army."

The prince thought for a moment, then answered that he would do such a thing.

In the early morning, the great armies of the sultan gathered in a battlefield. They were amazed when the single figure of the prince arrived on horseback. "We will slaughter him, for sure," they thought.

The prince, however, turned the key in the neck of the ebony horse and rose above the charging soldiers. They were so afraid, that they dropped their weapons and ran. The sultan, having seen what had happened, knew that the prince was a powerful figure. He agreed to allow him to marry his daughter.

Kamar al-Akmar returned to his father and his sisters with his new bride. He accused the Persian of playing a trick on him by not divulging where the second key was located on the ebony horse. The king, hearing this, and knowing that his son could have been carried away for good, banished the Persian from his court.

Then the king ordered the flying horse to be broken into a thousand pieces and discarded. The youngest princess rejoiced at her brother's saving actions. A great festival was held in honor of the prince and the bride he had found while flying on the ebony horse.

DESTRUCTION

How the World was Created, Destroyed, and Created Again

INDIA

The earth was shaped like a wheel. In the center of the world was Brahma's heaven. The heaven was called Mount Meru, and the mountain was 84,000 leagues high at its peak, or summit. The heaven was encircled by the River Ganges. The cities of Indra and the other gods surrounded it. The lower mountains, or the foothills, that scaled below Mount Meru were home to the Gandharvas, the good or benevolent spirits. The demons lived in the valleys.

The hood of the great serpent Shesha supported the whole world. When a great flood covered the universe, Shesha coiled up on the back of a tortoise. The world had many floods. At the end of each deluge, the world was born again.

Once, a golden cosmic egg glowed like fire and floated on the waters that buried the world. For a thousand years the lord of the universe brooded over the egg. Finally a lotus flower, as bright as a thousand suns, grew from his navel. The lotus spread and flourished until it contained the whole world. Brahma sprang from the lotus with the powers of the lord of the universe. He created the world from the parts of his body.

But, Brahma made some mistakes, and he had to learn from them. At first he created ignorance, and he tossed it away. But ignorance survived and became Night. From Night, the Beings of Darkness were born, and they set out to devour their creator.

"How can you eat your own father?" asked Brahma.

Some of the Beings of Darkness relented, but others did not soften in their desire to destroy Brahma. They became the Rakshasas, the enemies of men. Brahma learned from the experience, and he resolved to create immortal and heavenly beings. He brought to life four sages to finish his work. But the sages lost interest in the creation, and Brahma became angry. From his anger, Rudra sprang forth to complete the work.

When another flood covered the world, the world spirit threw a seed called Nara into the waters. Called Narayana after Nara, the first dwelling, the spirit grew inside the egg as Brahma. After one year, Brahma made his body into two parts. One half was male, and the other half was female.

Viraj, a male, grew inside the female half, and Viraj created Manu. Manu was a sage, called a Rishi. Manu lived ten thousand years in the worship of Brahma. He survived other floods, and he became equal to Brahma in his glory.

One day Manu was meditating beside a stream. A fish spoke to him from the water.

"Please, protect me from this fish that is chasing me," the fish begged Manu.

Manu put the fish into a pond. After some time, the fish grew too big for the pond.

"Please, place me into the River Ganges," requested the fish.

Manu did as the fish asked. But time passed, and the fish grew too large for the river.

"Please, take me to the ocean," implored the fish.

At last the fish was content. Manu learned that he had rescued none other than Brahma himself. Brahma warned Manu of the coming destruction of the world by a great flood.

"Build an ark and place in it the seven Rishis and the seeds of everything," Brahma instructed.

No sooner did Manu do as Brahma asked, when the deluge began. Everything in the world was blanketed by water once more. The ark tossed about upon the surface, and cables tied to the horns of the fish moved it along. Finally, Manu's ark rested upon the highest peak of the Himalayas, where Manu moored it to a tree.

The waters receded after many years, and Manu and the ark descended into the valleys. To prepare for the creation of the next age, Manu performed many sacrifices.

Manu offered up milk, clarified butter, curds, and whey to Brahma. He repeated the gesture every day. A year passed, and Manu's offering grew into a beautiful woman.

"I am your daughter," said the beautiful woman to Manu. "Together, we will perform other sacrifices to Brahma. As a result you will become rich in children and cattle. You will obtain any blessing you desire."

Manu did as his daughter said. They were true in their devotion to Brahma. In return, Manu fathered the human race, and he received many blessings.

Esu's Trick on the Two Friends

BRAZIL, CUBA, NIGERIA (YORUBA)

Esu was the gods' messenger. As messenger he brought the will of the gods down to humans. Because he was partly in the world of the gods and as much in the world of humans, his legs were of different lengths. This caused Esu to limp. In his arms he carried a clabash, or gourd, inside of which was the ase. The ase was the word of Olodumare, the Creator, when he made the universe.

Sometimes Esu played tricks on humans. This is the myth of the two friends and the trick Esu played on them. The two friends took a vow of eternal friendship. Esu heard them telling each other they would be friends forever, and he decided to do something about it. His plan was to test their friendship.

Esu made a cloth cap. The cap's right side was black. Its left side was white. He found the two friends tilling their land. One friend was hoeing on the right side of the field. The other friend was clearing bushes on the left side. In the middle of the field, riding between the men, was Esu, and on his head he wore the cap. The man on the right saw the black side of Esu's cap. Of course, the man who was clearing bushes saw the white side of the messenger's cap.

When it was time for lunch, the friends took a break from their labors in the field. They met in the cool shade of some trees as they always did.

"Did you see the man with the white cap who greeted us this morning while we worked? He was quite pleasant, don't you think?" said the friend who worked on the left side of the field.

"Yes, he was rather pleasant," answered the second friend. "But I recall him as a man in a black cap, not a white one."

"It was certainly a white cap. And the man rode a magnificently caparisoned horse."

"His horse was wonderfully decorated. It must be the same man. But I tell you, his cap was dark, and it was black," insisted the friend who had been hoeing on the right side of the field.

"Clearly, you are fatigued. Or the hot sun has blinded you. How else would you mistake a white cap for a black cap?" questioned the first friend.

"I tell you, it was black, and I am not mistaken. I can still see him," answered the second friend.

With that, the two men began to fight. So severe was their fighting that their neighbors came running from every direction to intervene. But they could do nothing to stop the fight. Into the middle of the uproar, Esu appeared. He was very calm, and he pretended not to know anything about what was happening.

Esu spoke harshly. "What is the meaning of this uproar?"

"Two close friends are fighting," said someone.

"They are about to kill each other," said someone else.

"And neither will tell us the cause of the fight," said a third person.

"Please, stop them," pleaded a fourth.

Esu scolded, "Why do you two lifelong friends make such a public spectacle of yourselves?"

The second friend tried to explain to Esu what had happened. "A man rode through the field and greeted us. He wore a black cap on his head. But my friend said it was a white cap and that I must have been tired or blind or both to think it was black."

"It was white," insisted the first friend.

"Both of you are right," offered Esu.

"How can that be possible?" demanded both friends at the same time.

"I am the man who paid the visit over which you both quarrel. And here is the cap that caused the commotion," said Esu. Out of his pocket he pulled the two-colored cap.

"As you can see," Esu continued, "one side is white, and the other side is black. You each saw one side. Therefore, you each are right in what you saw. Are you not the two friends who vowed to be friends forever?"

The friends shook their heads at what they saw and heard.

"When you vowed eternal friendship, you did not reckon with Esu," said the god. "Don't you know that he who does not put Esu first has himself to blame if things backfire?"

Some Ugly Gods Who Rewarded Humans

CHINA

Lei-kung was called My Lord Thunder. He was repulsively ugly! Not only was he shown with a blue body, but he had wings and claws, too. He dressed only in a loincloth. At his side he carried one or more drums. He carried a mallet and a chisel in his hands. He used the chisel to punish the guilty. Some say he used the mallet to create a drumroll of thunder. Others say he drove in the chisel with his mallet.

Lei-kung had orders from heaven to punish those humans who had committed a crime unpunishable by human laws. He often required the aid of humans to enact the punishment. Here is a myth about My Lord Thunder.

One day a hunter was eagerly in pursuit of game. A violent storm took him by surprise in the thick of the forest. The storm was punctuated by lightning and thunder so fierce in intensity that the hunter was terrified. The outbursts seemed to be at their strongest directly over a tree with uplifted branches. The strange tree was not far from where the frightened man stood.

When the hunter lifted his eyes, he saw something even stranger. In the tree was a

Lei-kung was called My Lord Thunder.

child holding a coarse flag. The flag was nothing more than a piece of filthy cloth tied to a splinter of wood.

My Lord Thunder also noticed the child. Just as the god was about to let loose a loud clap, the child waved the flag. Lei-kung suddenly stopped the outburst cold and retreated.

The hunter knew well that Lei-kung, like all gods, deplored things that were unclean. Such things were usually the work of an evil spirit. The man loaded his gun, raised it, and shot down the flag. Then Thunder struck the tree at once. The hunter was very close to the tree when Thunder struck, and he fainted.

When the man revived, he found a small roll of paper in his grasp. The message on the paper read: "Life prolonged for twelve years for helping with the work of heaven." The hunter then saw next to the shattered tree the grotesque corpse of an oversized lizard. He realized this to be the true form of the child he had seen with the filthy flag.

The god of Examination, named K'uei-hsing, was also one of the ugliest divinities in existence! He wore a constant grimace on his face. Bending forward, he held his left leg raised in a running posture while he propped himself on the head of a turtle called Ao. He carried a bushel basket in his left hand and a paintbrush in his right. With the paintbrush K'uei-hsing put a mark next to the names of the humans lucky enough to be chosen by the August Personage of Jade, Father-Heaven. In his bushel he measured the talents of all candidates. The god of Examination is a follower of the god of Literature, called Wen Ch'ang.

When the Chinese emperor gave an audience to scholars who passed their doctoral examinations, the emperor said, "May you alone stand on the head of Ao, the turtle that supported the god of Examination." What follows is a story about the student who took an examination.

The young student had worked hard in his preparation for the examination. The student, however, was not satisfied with his performance when he returned to his home. He knew that Wen Ch'ang and K'uei-hsing rewarded the efforts of hard work.

The student begged the gods to help him obtain good results from the examination. When the student slept, Wen Ch'ang appeared to him. In his dreams the student saw the god throw a bundle of examinations into a stove. The student saw his own test in the bundle. When the god removed the tests, they were entirely changed. Wen

Ch'ang handed the student his examination, and the student knew to study the changed material very carefully.

Upon waking, the student learned that a great fire had destroyed the examination building during the night, and all the tests were burned. Consequently, every examination candidate had to take the test again. With the new knowledge that the god had given him, the student passed with honors.

Creation from an Egg

JAPAN

In the days of old, heaven and earth were not yet separate. And the feminine, In, and masculine, Yo, were also not divided. Only a mass without form, but something like an egg, existed. The egg substance was without clear limits, and it contained germs.

One part of the egg was purer, and it became heaven. The heavier, grosser part settled down to become earth. The particles in the finer portion easily united to make heaven. The union of the grosser particles was accomplished with difficulty, which meant that heaven formed first.

Once heaven and earth were formed, Divine Beings were produced. It happened in this manner. When the world began to be created, the soil of the lands floated about like a fish floating on the surface of the water. In the realm between heaven and earth, the shoot of a reed took form. The reed transformed into a god. The god was called Kuni-toko-tachi no Mikoto, which meant Land-eternal-stand-of-august-thing. The god possessed majestic dignity.

There were seven generations of the age of the gods. Including Kuni-toko-tachi no Mikoto, eight deities in all were formed. They came into being by the mutual action of heaven and earth, and they were made male and female.

The last god and goddess to be formed were Izanagi no Mikoto, or Male-who-invites, and Izanami no Mikoto, Female-who-invites. Together they stood on the floating bridge of heaven and looked down.

"Is there not a country beneath?" they asked each other.

So they thrust the jewel-spear of heaven downward, and after some groping, they found the ocean. The brine that dripped from the spear's point coagulated and formed an island. They called the island Ono-goro-jima, or Spontaneously-congealed-island.

The two deities dwelled on the island. They stated their wish to become husband and wife and to produce countries. Ono-goro-jima became the pillar of the center of the land. By circling the pillar in opposite directions, and meeting at the same place, they were married.

Izanagi no Mikoto and Izanami no Mikoto began to produce islands. Their minds took no pleasure in the first they created. So they called the island Ahaji no Shima, or the island which is unsatisfactory. They tossed it away.

Next they produced the island of Oho-yamato no Toyo-aki-tsu-shima, or rich-harvest-of-island. The two islands of lyo no futa-na and Tsukusi followed. The twin islands Oki and Sado came next, as the precursors of the twin births that were to come later among humans.

The islands of Koshi, Oho-shima, and Kibi no ko were the sixth, seventh and eighth islands, which they created and kept. They called the country Oho-ya-shima. It meant great-eight-island country.

Two islands called Tsushima and Iki, along with some smaller islands, came into being afterward from the foam of the salt water. The two deities continued creating until they had made the sea, rivers, and mountains. Then they produced Ku-ku-no-chi, the ancestor of the trees, and Kaya no hime, the ancestor of herbs.

Izanagi no Mikoto and Izanami no Mikoto consulted each other. "We have made the great-eight-island country, the mountains, rivers, herbs, and trees. Shall we not produce someone who shall reign over the universe?"

In response, they produced the sun goddess. They called her Oho-hirume no muchi, or Great-noon-female-of-possessor. So resplendent was the sun goddess's luster that she shone throughout the six quarters of the North, South, East, West, Above, and Below.

Next they made the moon god as a companion to their wondrous daughter. He was as radiant as she was. And they sent the sun goddess and the moon god to rule in heaven.

Afterward they produced the leech-child. However, after three years, the leech-child could not stand upright. So they abandoned the child to the winds. The next child was Sosa no wo no Mikoto, called the Impetuous One, because this god possessed a fierce temper and was prone to cruelty. He caused great damage to the people and the lands of earth.

"You are exceedingly wicked. You are unfit to reign in the world. Therefore, depart to the land of Yomi, or Hades," said the two deities that created the Impetuous One. And they banished him to the Underworld.

Their next child was Kagu tsuchi, the god of fire. Kagu tsuchi burned her mother, Izanami no Mikoto. As she lay dying upon the earth, Izanami no Mikoto gave birth to the earth goddess and the water goddess. Kagu tsuchi, god of fire, and the earth goddess mated to produce a child named Waka-musubi, or young growth. Upon this god's head were produced the silkworm and the mulberry tree. In her navel were the five kinds of grain.

Quetzalcoatl

CENTRAL AMERICA AND MEXICO

Quetzalcoatl lived in Tollan in a great house constructed of gleaming silver. The house was surrounded by sweet gardens with flowers of every color of the rainbow. The fields of his land were filled with maize, or corn, that grew so tall that the stalks cast shadows on the full moon. The rooms of Quetzalcoatl's palace reflected the red of the mountain peaks, the greens and blues of turquoise stones, and the yellow of wildflowers. A thousand brightly colored birds flew among the clouds over his house and landed in the trees, where they sang songs to the people all day long.

The people of Tollan learned many useful crafts from Quetzalcoatl. He taught them about the stars and constellations of the skies. They learned how to work with silver and gems, how to build a house, how to paint and carve and sculpt. Everything they learned was taught in the spirit of peace, for Quetzalcoatl only shared the knowledge of things that were creative and beautiful. There was no war in Tollan, no fighting or jealousy or hunger.

Far away in the distant mountains, where the gray storm clouds rested from their long journey across the sky, there lived a sorcerer called Tezcatlipoca. Unlike Quetzalcoatl, he lived his life in pursuit of trouble and strife. He found pleasure in bringing heartache to others. Looking down from his dark perch, he sent a chilling, destructive wind into the valley where Quetzalcoatl's house was situated. The flowers in the garden felt the cold blast of air, closed their blooms and died.

Quetzalcoatl looked out the window of his silver house and saw what had occurred. His heart was filled with sadness. He called to one of his loyal servants and spoke to him.

"There is someone who wishes to harm me. If I am to protect this place, I must leave here today."

The servant was confused by Quetzalcoatl's words, though he packed some food for him and some warm blankets. Then he took many bags of precious jewels and gems and packed them, too. As the cold winds continued to blow, Quetzalcoatl left Tollan and went to the mountains. Several of his servants followed him.

As he traveled into the wilderness, he was tracked by a jaguar. He attempted to change his path many times to avoid the animal, but it was no use. The jaguar, who was really the evil Tezcatlipoca, had Quetzalcoatl's scent and was intent on hunting him.

Quetzalcoatl grew weary. He began to age, and the muscles of his arms and legs ached with fatigue. After he had crossed a great mountain range, he found a quiet valley, where he stopped for a while to rest. From one of the sacks, he took a mirror and looked at his reflection. Looking back at him was the face of an old, tired man. Homesick and discouraged, Quetzalcoatl threw the mirror into the tall grass. He thought of his beautiful home in Tollan, and the memories of it caused him to weep. His tears fell down upon the earth and left lasting marks on the stones.

The servants who accompanied him tried to raise his spirits by playing music on their flutes. For a time he forgot the bittersweet memories of his home and the constant sound of the jaguar who stalked him.

The sacks that Quetzalcoatl and his servants carried seemed to grow heavier and heavier with each mile they traveled. Quetzalcoatl decided to dump one of the sacks in the fountain Cozcaapan. It was the bag that contained his most precious treasures.

The men climbed higher and higher into another mountain range. It snowed and sleeted and hailed for days and nights. Eventually the loyal servants who had remained with Quetzalcoatl died from the bitter cold. He was left with only his memories and the taunting wind that came from the breath of Tezcatlipoca.

On the other side of the mountain, Quetzalcoatl found the sea. Upon seeing the great waters, he built a raft from snakes that he wove together. He sailed far away from the land, out into the middle of the ocean until he arrived in the land of Tlappallan, in the country of the sun. The jaguar spirit of Tezcatlipoca finally stopped pursuing him.

In Tlappallan he drank the waters of everlasting life and threw himself into a brightly burning fire. When the fire died, only the ashes of the kind and good Quetzalcoatl remained.

Some believe that Quetzalcoatl will return one day as a young, happy man, eager to teach the people of the world the good crafts of life, like weaving and spinning and painting and creating beautiful things. In the meantime his spirit appears as brightly colored birds, soaring and diving high above the treasure he cast in the fountain in the mountains.

Pele, Goddess of Fire

HAWAII

Beyond the crystal-blue waters of the Hawaiian islands, inside a crescent of warm white sand, is the great volcano Kilauea. It stands proud and tall, spitting fire and sparks at the sky. The people of the islands have long believed that the protector of the mountain Kilauea is Pele, the goddess of fire.

Like Kilauea, Pele was fiery and powerful. She could become angry quickly; nearly as quickly as the ocean could turn from calm to stormy. With her temper tantrums she could cause the volcano to spew forth hot, molten lava and poisonous gases. The people were afraid of Pele's moods and tried to appease her with sacrifices and music whenever they could.

One day Pele and her sisters and brothers were visiting the shores of the island. They relaxed in the golden sand. They collected shells and looked out at the deep, beautiful blue waters as graceful dolphins jumped in the foamy waves. Contented, Pele asked her favorite sister, Hiiaka, to watch over her as she slept. She spread a soft blanket in the sand and curled up to take a nap, while Hiiaka kept her cool by waving a palm leaf over her body.

Pele fell into a deep sleep. Soon the images of a dream called out to her. She dreamed of another island, not far from her own. The people on the island were dancing and celebrating. They feasted on wonderful food. They danced the hula. In the middle of the dancing, Pele saw a beautiful young man, who had commanded the attention of all the women around him. She was astounded by his skill as a dancer, and his graceful motions.

Without waking, Pele turned herself into a spirit and went to find the handsome man of her dreams. Hiiaka kept fanning her sister, believing that she was enjoying her sleep. She didn't know that Pele was traveling away from the peaceful seashore, toward another island.

Pele's spirit came to the island in her dreams. There she found the prince of Kauai, as tall and graceful as she remembered him to be. Pele changed herself into a beautiful, young woman and approached the prince.

"Prince Lohiau," she said to him, "I have come here to dance with you."

The prince, not knowing that the woman was really the goddess Pele, said to her, "Welcome to my island. I am glad you are here. Please, know that I must dance with all of the young women here."

Pele was not pleased with Lohiau's words. She had hoped that he would find her more beautiful than any other woman. She cast a spell on him so that he could not resist her charms. The spell worked its magic. Prince Lohiau fell in love with Pele.

Pele spent many days with the prince as his wife. They were happy together. However, Pele knew that she had to return to the volcano and her sisters and brothers. One day she told Lohiau that she had some errands to take care of in another land, but would return to him as soon as they were completed. She bid him good-bye and went on her way.

Many, many days passed and Pele did not return to her husband as she said she would. The prince grew weak with sadness. His people tried to cheer him up, but it was hopeless. He refused to eat or drink. He would not leave his house. Finally he crawled into his bed and died of a broken heart.

Pele had returned to the spot where she had been taking a nap under the watchful eyes of her sister Hiiaka. When she woke, she told her sister of the dream in which she fell in love with the Prince Lohiau.

"I have heard that the prince is dead," Hiiaka told her sister. "Some say he was in love with a beautiful woman who left him, and he died of a broken heart."

Pele was moved by the story Hiiaka told. "If this is true, Sister," she said, "then you must travel to the land of the dead and bring him back to me, for I am the one that he loved."

Hiiaka did not understand Pele's words, but she did as she was asked. She went to the fiery underworld to find Lohiau. Many months passed before she succeeded in finding the prince and restoring him to life.

Lohiau was grateful to Hiiaka. He was touched by her kindness and her devotion to her sister Pele. Hiiaka explained that it was Pele who wished for him to return to her in Hawaii. He left the land of death with Hiiaka.

Just as they were approaching the beautiful shores of the home of Hiiaka, the two saw a terrible sight. The volcano Kilauea had erupted many times. The sands of the beach where Hiiaka loved to walk were covered with black, smoking lava. The trees were scorched and burned; all the brightly colored flowers that grew on the hillsides had been reduced to ash.

Hiiaka knew that this was the handiwork of her sister Pele. She approached Pele and asked her why she had done such a thing.

"I thought that you would never return," Pele replied, embarrassed at her own jealousy. "I thought you might fall in love and keep him for your own."

"I cannot understand your cruelty to your sister!" Lohiau cried out loud to Pele. "She risked all kinds of danger to find me among the dead. She was always kind and good to me."

Pele thought about her actions. She asked Lohiau and Hiiaka to forgive her. "The land will soon return to its former glory," she told them. "The trees and flowers will grow back. The sand will become white again. Let us celebrate tonight that you have returned safely, and I will be content that you are alive, Lohiau."

That night there was a great festival on the island. Torches burned brightly into the night and the people all danced and sang in joyous celebration. Lohiau danced the hula for Hiiaka, and even Pele remained calm and content, happy that she had been forgiven for her terrible temper.

The Search for Fire

YANA TRIBE, NATIVE AMERICAN

In the beginning of time the Yana people of Clover Creek had fire, but it was only in the form of a glowing ember—warm, but not very hot. They could not cook the meat of the animals that they hunted, nor could they see very far in the dark.

Au Mujaupa was a powerful god who was the master of fire. But he kept the secret of the flames to himself. He lived in the south of the land, far away, across the currents of a powerful river.

One day a member of the Yana tribe named Gray Wolf decided to depart from his village in search of the fire that could roast venison and cure fish. He traveled to the peak of Lassen's Butte, which was called Wahkanopa. High above the land, he looked out into the darkness for flames that might belong to Au Mujaupa. There was no sign of fire in any direction. He returned home.

The chief of the village advised Gray Wolf to climb to the top of Mount Shasta for a better view of the world. He introduced Gray Wolf to Sigwegi, or "Little Bird," who had a remarkable gift of sight that allowed him to see through trees and even down to the core of the earth.

The two men climbed Mount Shasta. In the evening they looked to the north, the east, and the west in hopes of finding Au Mujaupa's fire. There was nothing but darkness, and a few stars.

Then they looked toward the south. Suddenly Gray Wolf spied a small orange glow in the distance.

"I think I see fire!" he said to Little Bird.

"I see it, as well, Gray Wolf!" Little Bird replied.

The men descended Mount Shasta and returned to their people. Gray Wolf addressed the chief.

"Little Bird and I have seen where Au Mujaupa keeps his fire. It is far away and to the south of this land. We will need many people to recover it."

Fifty people volunteered to go with the men. The journey to the south was long and very difficult. By the time they reached the outskirts of Au Mujaupa's village, there were only three people left in the expedition: Gray Wolf, Metsi, and Shushu Marima, the old woman.

Au Mujaupa kept the fire in a large sweathouse in the middle of his village. The fire was guarded by several powerful warriors; among them were Patcha ("Snow"), Chil Wareko ("Big Rain"), and the winds of the four directions.

When the people of Au Mujaupa's village were fast asleep, Gray Wolf, Metsi, and Shushu crept silently toward the sweathouse. They climbed onto the roof, and Gray Wolf went inside to hand out pieces of the fire to his friends. Gray Wolf gave them to Shushu first, who put them in her ears for safekeeping. Then he gave some to Metsi. After filling his own ear with pieces from Au Mujaupa's fire, Gray Wolf and the other two stole away in the night.

Not long after they had left the sweathouse, Au Mujaupa woke from his sleep. He quickly noticed that the fire pile in the center of his hut had been disturbed.

"Someone has stolen my fire!" he cried to his guards. Au Mujaupa did not want anyone else to possess the powerful element of fire. The guards jumped up from their sleep and began to pursue the three. Chil Wareko drenched them with torrents of rain. Patcha covered them with biting frost, and the winds blew gales at them.

Metsi became so frozen that the fires in his ears were extinguished. Gray Wolf's fire died, as well. But Shushu kept her hand over one ear. She managed to prevent the fire from going out. Several pieces fell to the earth from her other ear. Au Mujaupa's guards found the pieces and thought they had foiled the thieves from leaving with fire.

Gray Wolf and Metsi struggled back to the village, leaving Shushu trailing behind. When they arrived, they explained to the chief and his people that they were not able to prevent the guards from recovering the precious pieces of fire that they carried in their ears. The people were disappointed.

"Where is Shushu?" the chief asked the two men.

"I am afraid she is frozen dead," Gray Wolf solemnly replied.

That evening as the village gathered in the hut of the chief, a person appeared out of the dark shadows. It was Shushu, frozen and nearly dead.

She walked to the center of the hut and shook her head over a pile of wood dust. Soon the pieces of fire she had stored in her ear fell onto the dust and ignited it. Excitedly the villagers scrambled about to bring more wood to the beautiful golden flames that were lighting the interior of the hut. The fire grew and grew.

The people then selected pieces of red meat and roasted them in the flames. The cold meat became hot and sweet. There was a great feast for many days, and all of the villagers returned to their huts with pieces of the flame that Shushu had so bravely stolen from the sweathouse of Au Mujaupa.

Illustration Credits

Bibliotheque des Arts Decoratifs, Paris, France/Bridgeman Art Library: p. 58

"Trojan Horse" by Tamas Galambos/Bridgeman Art Library: p. 35

Corbis: p.12

W. M. Cuthill: p. 164

Mary Hamilton Frye: p. 47

Erich Lessing/Art Resource, NY: p.93

Mary Evans Picture Library: pp. 14, 25, 30, 31, 52, 63, 147, 156,160, 174

National Museum and Gallery of Wales, Cardiff/Bridgeman Art Libary: p. 71

Willy Pogany: p.138

READ ALOUD LIBRARY